**Other Books by Scott Corbett**

*We Chose Cape Cod*
*Cape Cod's Way*
*The Sea Fox*

FOR YOUNG CHILDREN

*Susie Sneakers*

# MIDSHIPMAN CRUISE

# Midshipman Cruise

*by*
*Scott*
*Corbett*

*An Atlantic Monthly Press Book*
**Little, Brown and Company**
*Boston • Toronto*

ATLANTIC–LITTLE, BROWN BOOKS
ARE PUBLISHED BY
LITTLE, BROWN AND COMPANY
IN ASSOCIATION WITH
THE ATLANTIC MONTHLY PRESS

Published simultaneously in Canada
by Little, Brown & Company (Canada) Limited

PRINTED IN THE UNITED STATES OF AMERICA

*To Charles W. Morton,*
*Destroyerman by Adoption*

# PREFACE

This story is based on the Midshipman Training Cruise to Northern Europe. As a civilian guest aboard a destroyer during the two months of the cruise, I became very fond of the officers, the crew, the midshipmen, and the tough little ship herself, and enjoyed every one of the more than 14,000 steaming miles we covered together.

My special thanks must go to the following:

To Charles W. Morton, the Associate Editor of the *Atlantic Monthly,* who first suggested that a cruise with the Navy might be arranged, and charted my course in the right direction;

To Commander Eric S. Purdon, the Navy's public information officer in Boston, who thought of making it the Midshipman Training Cruise;

To Commander Richard M. Niles, skipper of the U.S.S. *N. K. Perry;* Lieutenant Commander William W. Therriault, executive officer; and to every officer and enlisted man aboard her on the cruise;

To Lieutenant Warren C. Graham, Jr., and Lieutenant (jg) Ben L. Bowden, officers-in-charge of the midshipmen aboard the *N. K. Perry;*

To Midshipman James W. Bibb USNA and all the other midshipmen who helped me in so many ways every day of the cruise.

SCOTT CORBETT

*East Dennis, Mass.*

# MIDSHIPMAN CRUISE

# CHAPTER I

MIDSHIPMAN NELSON CRANE stared glumly ahead through the sheets of rain that were pockmarking Chesapeake Bay and wished he had sat beside someone with less enthusiasm. The tall, gangly third classman next to him was being far too cheerful about everything. He had a farmboy's face, bony and long of nose, and his accent was pure prairie.

In all, forty-nine Annapolis midshipmen sat on the thwarts of the big open motor launch enduring a rough, wet ride. The black rain-covers on their caps and the long black rain capes which enveloped them gave the middies the solemn uniformity of a boatload of penguins.

The uniformity was misleading, since two classes were represented, first and third. The third classmen were men who had just finished their first, or plebe, year, and were entering their second. The first classmen had finished their third, and were about to begin their final year of training at the United States Naval Academy.

"By the way, my name's Tomlinson," declared the cheerful hayseed.

3

"Crane."

"First name's Oscar."

"Nelson," said Nels, and found his hand being firmly gripped and shaken by a huge set of rawboned fingers. Though both third classmen, they had not met before. A thousand Annapolis third classmen and nearly as many first classmen were going on the cruise. Few of the men in the motor launch had known each other personally before being thrown together for the trip.

"Glad to know you, Nelson."

"Nels for short."

"Okay, Nels for short. Isn't this great, us getting the *Morton?* She's supposed to be the best can on the cruise. I understand she has an E, and a first-rate skipper. I sure was lucky anyway. I wanted a destroyer, but they had me down for one of the heavies, and then at practically the last minute I was switched to a tin can."

"Depends on what you call luck," said Nels. A heavy — a battleship or cruiser — was exactly what he had wanted. He wondered darkly if his father, an old destroyer man, or his big brother, Perry, at present the operations officer aboard a destroyer, had had anything to do with his being stuck on a can.

Nels wanted no part of the small ships. For one thing, he was not sure he would be a good sailor, and seasickness was practically unheard of on the smooth-riding heavies. For another thing, there would be more places to get lost aboard a heavy, and he intended to goof off as much as possible. He was taking the cruise to satisfy his father, to

4

fulfill a bargain; but that didn't mean he had to work too hard at it.

As far as Nels was concerned, he was about to waste two months of his life. A year at the Academy had not changed his opinion of the Navy. Everything that happened seemed only to add fuel to the fire. That last-minute incident, for example, as he was walking down the steps of Bancroft Hall with his OAO (One and Only, as they were called at Annapolis).

Nels's OAO, Eloise Murdoch, had been complaining again.

"Of all days, why did it have to rain today? I must look awful!"

Like hundreds of other girls who had come to see the midshipmen embark, Eloise had received several drenchings during the long delay the weather had caused. Her hair looked as though she had just surfaced in a swimming pool, her shoes squelched as she walked, and her mouth was a sulky rosebud.

Still, she was actually a very pretty girl, and when she was not complaining or worrying about her clothes and her hair and her make-up she could be Nels's idea of the only girl in the world. He put his arm around her and gave her a quick squeeze.

"Never mind, Eloise, you look wonderful to me."

"I may look wonderful to you, but I probably look like a wet mouse to the rest of them," she declared unhappily. "And you'd better be careful."

5

"I took my arm away quick, didn't I?"

"Yes, but watch out — that old fusspot may still be running around taking names."

"Never mind Sticky, I haven't seen him for five minutes. Things are in such a mess around here he can't catch up with everybody."

The Naval Academy had intended to embark its midshipmen for their summer training cruise at 0600 that morning. Rain and rough water on Chesapeake Bay had held up the operation. The Navy was capable of putting the men aboard at any time, but in the tight quarters of small ships it was desirable to have them arrive relatively dry. During the long wait that had ensued, nearly two thousand midshipmen, with their families and their girl friends, had been turned back into Dahlgren Hall for shelter and, eventually, an improvised luncheon.

At 1300, embarkation was to proceed in spite of the weather. Midshipmen were saying good-by to their girls on all sides of Nels and Eloise. Third classmen were not supposed to kiss girls or even put their arms around them on the steps of Bancroft Hall, not even while saying good-by for two months, but in the confusion of the moment some of Nels's classmates were taking chances.

"Arm around young lady! Name!"

A bustling Navy officer had suddenly appeared, followed by a third classman carrying a pad and pencil. Somebody had to think about discipline, even in that dark hour, and Lieutenant Leo ("Sticky") Stickney was temperamentally suited to be that man. His finger, pointed accusingly,

6

caused Nels to snap to attention so stiffly that one could all but hear his muscles twang.

"Midshipman Nelson Crane, third class, sir."

"Crane, I'm placing you on report for the specified offense. You will appear at midshipmen's mast before youɪ officer-in-charge during the cruise."

"Aye aye, sir."

The third classman scribbled, and Lieutenant Stickney departed. Eloise sputtered.

"But you *didn't* have your arm around me! Not now, anyway. You only had hold of my arm, helping me down the steps."

"I know, but he must have seen me the other time — or some other officer told him."

"Well, I don't think that's fair!"

"It's the Navy. That's why —" Nels began, and then bit his lip. He had almost said, "That's why I'm getting out."

While Nels brooded over this latest unpleasantness, the long, low, rakish outlines of destroyers rolling at anchor rent the wet gray curtain ahead of them, swung past them, and disappeared into the wet gray curtain behind them as the motor launch labored through choppy seas. A fresh-water drizzle and salt-water spray combined to keep the middies well dampened down. Then at last they rounded a low stern with *Morton* lettered on it, and slowed for an approach on the port quarter. A sea ladder was over the side, and an officer and a few men were standing by.

The officer, Ensign William Faye, looked down with the

7

weary gaze of an old sea dog and groaned at the thought of having to teach this boatload of green kids the ways of the sea for the next two months. Annapolis was a whole year in the past for him, and he had already made a tough four months' cruise to the Mediterranean.

Up on the fo'c'sle, Bosun's Mate First Class Ernie Bangs squinted along the side of the ship for a look at the new arrivals, and then dropped back through the hatch to the bosun's locker with a puckery grin on his round face. Officer material, were they? Well, maybe they'd be working the tail off him someday, but for the next two months it would be the other way around.

The instant the motor launch was secured alongside the ladder, midshipmen began to scramble onto deck. Despite the difficulty of struggling up the heaving ladder with their arms thrust awkwardly through slits in their bulky rain capes, most of them managed the proper routine—the salute aft to the flag, the salute to the officer of the deck, and the words, "Sir, I request permission to come aboard." Nels took his turn up the ladder, with Oscar Tomlinson behind him, and at that moment a heavy canvas bag full of navigation textbooks was passed up out of the launch. Nels took the bag with one big hand, hunched his broad shoulders, and swung it above him onto the deck.

If Ensign Faye had worn size eight shoes, all might have been well, but he wore size elevens. The extra length was fatal.

"Ow-w-wow!" yelled Mr. Faye, and went into an interest-

8

ing little dance of indecision. He couldn't make up his mind which set of toes to massage first.

"Gee, sorry, sir! Er — request p-permission to come aboard, sir," stammered Nels, saluting in various directions.

"Dammit! Permission granted. Reluctantly," added Mr. Faye.

"Aye aye, sir," said Nels, and scuttled away in the direction indicated by a grinning sailor. Mr. Faye glared after Nels and made a mental note.

Nels hurried forward through a confusing array of first impressions that assaulted all his senses at once. Most of all he was immediately conscious of the roaring sound that makes a destroyer seem a living, snorting being as long as the noise persists, and a very dead thing if it suddenly stops. The engines, tubes, blowers, intakes — all the arteries and veins and lungs and heart of a warship — combined at all times, at anchor or under way alike, to fill every space and corner of the ship with a throbbing roar.

From the galley a sturdy whiff of cooking sent him greetings. Under his feet the steel deck felt slippery and treacherous whenever he strayed from the abrasive treads. And he barked his instep on the first door he stepped through.

The crew's forward living quarters had been cleared for the midshipmen. Some of the crew had been off-loaded to make room for them, and would rejoin the ship after the cruise. The remainder were jammed into the after living quarters, and didn't like it.

The midshipmen's compartments were two levels below the main deck, under the mess deck. The bunks were in three tiers, each bunk tagged with a middie's name. The men poured down into their new home in jostling, chattering confusion and sought out the pipe bunks, suspended by chains, that were to provide such sleep as they would manage to get during the next two months. On the canvas bottom of one turned-up bunk a word of welcome had been printed in chalk by some member of the crew:

WELCOME, MIDDIES
FOR TWO YEARS WE'VE SERVED OUR TIME IN
HELL, YOURS IS YET TO COME

"Free verse," remarked Oscar.

"The Voice of Experience," said Nels.

Oscar examined a name tag. "I understand the idea is to mix us all up, first class and third class, Academy and NROTC."

"Just crazy mixed-up kids, that's us. Well, anyway, here's mine." Nels had spotted his name on a middle bunk in a corner.

"And what do you know — there's mine, right above yours," Tomlinson announced cheerfully. "Looks like we're bunkmates, ol' buddy."

"Is this what they call mixing us up?" muttered Nels. Now, on top of everything else, he was stuck with a hayseed eager beaver. Oscar had not heard what he said, however. Oscar had found something new to be pleased about.

"A top bunk, too. That's a break."

"What's so good about a top bunk?"

The gangly lad cocked a twinkling eye his way.

10

"I'll explain that later. Come on, let's sneak out of here for a while and go topside — I want to watch 'em weigh anchor."

Oscar Tomlinson had a way of hustling a fellow along almost before he knew what was happening to him. Nels found himself hurrying along just as though he gave a darn whether they hauled up the anchor or dropped it into the bay for good.

"Well, it passes the time," he growled to himself as he followed Oscar up on deck.

The ship was astir now, waiting only for orders from the division commander to get under way. The men assigned to anchor detail were breaking out the hoses used to wash off the chain and anchor as they were heaved in. A talker wearing an S/P (sound-powered) telephone headset stood ready to relay orders from the bridge. Mr. Faye, being first division officer, was on hand, and stood near the rail talking to a grizzled CPO who was the *Morton's* chief bosun's mate. Nearer at hand, a bosun's mate first class who was pot-bellied and yet still undeniably hard-muscled and certainly a tough customer was ambling about the deck giving orders. His orders included a number of four-letter words not to be found in *The Bluejackets' Manual,* but he got things done. As the midshipmen appeared and stood in front of the forward five-inch gun mount, Mount 51, he glanced over his meaty shoulder and noticed them. Ernie Bangs folded his arms and grinned his puckery grin.

" 'Tenshun on deck, men! Here's two of our young gentlemen."

Oscar had been gawking around like a bumpkin in New York City getting his first look at the tall buildings, but now he turned and smiled his slow, friendly smile.

"Hope we're not in the way. We want to see if you can haul that anchor up in one piece," he explained.

"Oh, I see. First cruise, huh?"

"First time I've even been aboard a real ship."

"No kidding?" Bangs threw his buddies a wink. "Well, we better begin right at the beginning, then. Now this here front porch part, this is called the bow, and that back part there, that's called the stern —"

"Oh, we got that far back at school, all right," Oscar assured him. "Matter of fact, I was just noticing this can's got twin fives instead of single barrels, and extra radar equipment on the mast and one thing and another, and I've just about concluded this isn't an ordinary destroyer at all, but actually one of the 711 class long-hull destroyers fitted out as a radar picket. But getting back to nomenclature, why don't you try us on ground tackle?" he suggested, giving tackle the proper "tay-kul" pronunciation. "For instance, the chain comes up through the hawsepipe, goes around the wildcat on the windlass here, and down through the chain pipe into the chain locker, and that stopper with the pelican hook on it is shackled to a pad eye; but what do you call that black cover on the chain pipe, and what do you call the padding inside it — the jackass, or the Dutchman?"

Bangs spit over the side without even shifting his feet, and jerked a thumb at Oscar. "This kid is real cool. What about your buddy — he all sharpened up, too? What's that little patch of deck called up there where the bows come to a point, now?"

"The eyes of the ship," said Nels.

"And what else? There's a little ol' plate set in the deck there with F.P. stamped onto it. What do you figure that to stand for — fire plug?"

"No — forepeak."

"Well, what do you know? Say, I sure hope you boys can work as good as you talk, because we're gonna need more than talk around here now that they've off-loaded half our best men to make room for you squirts —"

*"Stand by to weigh anchor!"* called the talker, and idle chatter ceased as all hands readied for action. One man stood by the jack that fluttered soggily from the jack staff, ready to haul it down the instant the ship got under way. Others turned on the two hoses and began to play them on the chain at the water's surface.

*"Up anchor!"*

The man at the controls started the windlass. The chain began to crawl up through the hawsepipe and across the deck. As soon as the chief bosun's mate, leaning far out to watch, reported the anchor in sight, the ship began to move.

"Ol' buddy," said Oscar, unashamedly thrilled, "we're on our way to Europe. Think of it!"

"You think of it. For Pete's sake, Tomlinson, we're still only on our way down the bay to Norfolk to pick up a mess of Rotsies," snorted Nels.

"Well, yes, I did forget about the ROTC boys. We do have that one stop to make — but after that . . ."

Horrible curses rose from below decks. The chain had fouled in the chain locker and was piling up in the pipe.

"Hit the brake!" yelled Bangs. The anchor chain halted. Mr. Faye sprang forward and betrayed his inexperience. His only thought was to clear the chain, and to do that it would have to be run back up out of the locker.

"Let the chain run," he ordered. The anchor began to drop again. At the rail, the old chief nearly jumped overboard.

"You can't do *that,* sir, you'll have the anchor catching bottom! Hold it!"

"Er — hit the brake!" agreed Mr. Faye, on second thought. A stopper was fastened to the anchor chain to hold it where it was, and only then was the chain in the locker run out on deck and cleared. But by then, to the last man, the anchor detail was red-necked and mortified.

"Gee-hosaphat! If that anchor had found bottom again, I'm here to bet it'd have been like a man stumbling over his own feet," whispered Oscar. He glanced at Bangs and cleared his throat.

"Well, we'll leave you to your work," he declared gently. "Come on, Crane, we better go below before someone misses us."

"Right, Tomlinson. I think we've learned all we can here," said Nels, and they turned away, with a year of plebe discipline going into the making of their straight faces. Only when they were through the hatchway did Oscar's whinny get away from him.

Bangs and Mr. Faye exchanged dark glances.

14

"Guess I'll have to take charge of that skinny young cornball," growled Bangs.

"That's all right with me, so long as you leave the other one," snapped Mr. Faye. "That one's *mine.*"

At the Norfolk Navy Yard the destroyers of the *Morton's* division were nested alongside a pier, all four lashed together side by side. Everywhere one looked there were other destroyers, or big tubby tenders, or submarines, and in the distance rose the masts of the majestic battleships *Iowa* and *New Jersey* and cruisers *Macon* and *Des Moines.* These four ships, with sixteen destroyers and two oilers, were to make up the task group that comprised the fleet for Cruise Able.

At Norfolk, over a thousand Naval Reserve Officers Training Corps (NROTC) midshipmen from twenty-five universities came aboard the ships. Twenty-two of them joined the forty-nine Annapolis men already aboard the *Morton.* Of the total group, forty were first classmen, and thirty-one were third classmen.

Over six hundred midshipmen were aboard each battleship, and nearly four hundred on each cruiser. The oilers were auxiliary ships, and carried no midshipmen.

All the Naval Academy's first and third classmen went on Cruise Able, but only part of the NROTC midshipmen.

In all, fifty-two universities had NROTC units. Later in the summer, other cruises, Cruise Baker and Cruise Charlie, would take the remainder of the NROTC midshipmen to

15

the Mediterranean, in the case of Baker, and to the Caribbean, in the case of Charlie.

The fleet remained at Norfolk for two days, while the NROTC men and additional supplies came aboard. And at 0750 of their first morning at Norfolk, Mr. Faye thought of something for Nels to do.

"Crane!" snapped Mr. Faye, noting his presence on deck. He had no difficulty learning Nels's name, since it was stenciled in block letters across the chest of his whites.

"Yes, sir?"

"Take this jack forward and stand by for Colors."

"Aye aye, sir."

"And see that you do it smartly."

"Aye aye, sir."

"And that doesn't mean smart-alecky. We don't like wise guys aboard the *Morton,* understand?"

"Aye aye, sir."

With the jack under his arm, Nels walked forward to the jack staff. This was all pretty childish. Any idiot could snap a flag onto a halyard and run it up when a whistle blew. He snapped the flag into place and stood ready. At 0800 sharp, whistles sounded on every side and flags went up all over the yard. None went up more smartly than Nels's.

As he came aft, Mr. Faye appeared again.

"Crane, I've just spoken to your officer-in-charge. Bangs needs a couple of midshipmen for a little project, and I couldn't think of a better pair to ask for than you and your friend Tomlinson."

Another callow effort on Mr. Faye's part, thought Nels

16

with a weary inward sigh. He regarded the officer woodenly.

"Aye aye, sir."

Two minutes later Nels and Oscar were beginning, under Bangs's glinting eye, what was to be a long and steady acquaintance with a small iron bar that was one of the Navy's favorite tools — the paint-chipper. On a destroyer, somebody was always either chipping old paint off or putting new paint on, and during the midshipmen's cruise that somebody was usually a third classman. For the next two months, the tapping and banging and clanking of the paint chippers was to be an almost constant *motif* in the cacophonous symphony of ship sounds.

Four minutes later the chief bosun's mate on the *Wareham*, the destroyer next to the *Morton*, spotted something that only an old Navy hand would have noticed. He strutted to the rail like a turkey cock and called across in a gravelly voice that was hoarse with scorn.

"Hey, you got yer jack upside down!"

All eyes on the fo'c'sle of the *Morton* turned toward the six rows of eight white stars on a blue field that waved from the jack staff. It was humiliating to think that another ship's chief bosun's mate, now swaggering away so arrogantly, should have been the one to notice that all forty-eight little five-pointed stars were pointing downward.

"Crane!" bellowed young Mr. Faye in a tone that made Nels's paint-chipper clatter to the deck. As the Navy expression puts it, Mr. Faye was shook.

"Oh, boy!" Nels groaned to Oscar as he scrambled to his feet. "Now I'll *never* get him off my back!"

17

# CHAPTER II

THE SORTIE from Chesapeake Bay into the open sea was given the full antisubmarine treatment, with the two squadrons of destroyers screening the heavies and scouring the immediate area for lurking subs.

Twelve destroyers in a column of twos led the way. At the mouth of the bay each ship in both columns turned out in a bottom search for seventy-five hundred yards, while the extra division, four destroyers abreast, raced up through the center of the column. The twelve ships doubled back, meshed in a crossing, went seventy-five hundred yards out again, and took up stations in a horseshoe screen.

Out came the heavies in a column of twos, first the cruisers abreast, then the battleships, and finally the oilers. Moving up fast, they took stations in the center of the ring, while behind them the destroyers closed in, in a circular screen.

In this way began fifteen days at sea — fifteen days during which, if all went well, the screws of twenty-two war-

18

ships would never once stop turning, day or night, until the ships reached their Northern European ports.

Amidships on the superstructure deck of the *Morton* — an upper deck more commonly referred to as "the O-1 level" — a large magazine which was normally crammed with ammunition for the three-inch 50's had been cleared out and turned into a workroom for the midshipmen navigators. In front of this "nav shack," as it was called, Lieutenant Henry Clay Jackson had gathered his charges together for a few introductory remarks.

Mr. Jackson was as Southern as his name, and so was his accent. An Academy graduate himself, he was currently doing a tour of duty there as an instructor in seamanship and navigation. He had seen considerable sea duty, had commanded a minesweeper, and was reputed to know his business.

As officer-in-charge of the midshipmen unit aboard the *Morton,* he had one assistant, a lieutenant junior grade who was an NROTC instructor at one of the universities.

Nels stood on the fringe of the group and appraised Mr. Jackson with a discouraged expression. Mr. Jackson looked like all the other instructors at the Academy — strong for regulations, everything by the numbers. No matter what they were like before, they always got that way the minute they started teaching at the Academy. Gimlet eyes, and a vocal delivery like Moses handing down the Ten Commandments. Now hear this, now hear this: thou shalt not . . . Moses with a Southern accent. Nels hastily wiped a grin off his face.

". . . I want to tell you all you're mighty lucky to be on this ship, because this is one of the best cans in the Navy. I had first pick of destroyers when we were settin' up for this cruise, and I picked the *Morton*," Mr. Jackson was saying. "Furthermore, we're going to hit the best ports. So you can feel mighty lucky. Now, as to general conduct, I want to tell you all a few things I will not tolerate. First off, I will not tolerate any friction with the crew. Now you're going to be livin' close with them, and you third classmen are going to be eatin' at the same tables with 'em, and I want you to get along. Remember, these white hats are the backbone of the Navy, and you can learn a lot from them. Also, I will not tolerate any back talk from third classmen to first classmen — just remember that they're your officers, and . . ."

Mr. Jackson had lost Nels again. Nels was thinking about how often his father had spoken with a sort of exasperated affection of the "white hats," the enlisted men of the Navy. He was thinking about his father, and his brother Perry, and the way they had talked Navy until it ran out of his ears every time they had one of their rare family get-togethers.

He could never understand how his father could love so much anything that had caused him such pain and heartbreak. A man who everybody said would have made admiral had been decorated, promoted to captain — and retired, because of the limp and the cane that a Korean shore battery had left him with. How could he accept that so uncomplainingly? The gallantry and courage he had displayed had brought his naval career to its shining peak — and also ended it. A brilliant victory had cost him his brilliant future, because it had left him short of the minimum physical requirements for a naval officer. How could he love the Navy? Nels, a boy of twelve when it happened, could not. He could only resent the Navy fiercely, and determine never to have anything to do with it.

And yet, when the time came . . . It was crazy, the way the big things that happened in a fellow's life, the big decisions, never seemed to hinge on large-scale, careful consideration, but on some little, fleeting incident. Nels could remember exactly the moment when he had given in, when he had surrendered, when he had agreed inside himself to try for an appointment to the Naval Academy, and it had all hinged on the set of his father's shoulders, the fading gleam in his eye, and the crease on his wrist as the cane took his weight.

At first, when the possibility of an appointment began to be mentioned with such studied casualness, Nels had come out hard against the mere thought of it. No argument, nothing his father said, nothing Perry had said — all but taking him by the ear while he said it — had been able to move him. All had been well until that fatal moment when his father had given up, graciously and uncomplainingly, and Nels had realized he was giving up his most precious dream.

He could remember every detail of his room that day, the exact way the sunlight cut across his desk as he sat staring fiercely out the window, the exact way his father had

21

tapped on his door and come in clearing his throat. "Now, look here, son, I don't want you sitting in here making yourself unhappy about this. You've got a right to make up your own mind about anything as big as this, and if you don't want the Academy, then that's that. So let's forget about it. I consider the subject closed."

He could feel again the brief touch on his shoulder, warm and reassuring, and see again the way his father had turned and left the room. As he watched him go, briskly in spite of his limp, something had seemed to give way inside Nels, and he found himself saying to himself, *I can't refuse that man anything.* It wasn't just because his father had been denied so much else he had once hoped for, either. It certainly wasn't pity, because there was a splendid jaunty quality about his father, an undimmed cheerfulness, that would have made pity preposterous.

". . . So we're going to pass out these cruise journal instructions, now, and I expect every man to take good care of his copy," Mr. Jackson was saying. The groan that had greeted some previous reference to cruise journals had recaptured Nels's attention. A sternly raised hand stifled the outburst. "Now, I don't want to hear any gripin' and groanin' about your cruise journals, because they aren't a quarter the size of the ones we had last year. I'll agree they were a little heavy last time, and I can see you've heard a lot about 'em, but we've cut the journal 'way down this year and there's no reason you all won't be able to keep 'em right up to snuff without strainin' your milk any, and I expect you all to do just that."

22

The cruise journal instructions comprised a sheaf of mimeographed assignments, questions to be answered in writing, which dealt with the three phases of naval science — gunnery, navigation and operations, and engineering — that they would be studying. Both classes of midshipmen were divided into three groups, each group to study the three phases in rotation during the cruise. Phase I for Nels's group was Navigation and Operations; Phase II, Engineering; and Phase III, Gunnery.

Nels thumbed through the instructions and grumbled with the rest. The sheets seemed to be full of tiresome queries and suggestions, such as:

Describe the path of the 3"/50 Cal. ammunition train from a below-deck magazine to the hopper of a topside gun mount.

What safety precautions must be observed in the operation of a $CO_2$ smothering system in the paint locker?

Describe briefly procedure for blowing tubes. Include who initiates action, who gives permission to blow tubes, and how often tubes should be blown. What is result if tubes are not blown for a long period?

"Somebody blows his stack," Nels muttered by way of answering the last question. He glanced at Oscar, who, as he usually seemed to be, was standing beside him, and added, "This really is for the birds."

"Oh, I don't know." Oscar was reading intently. "Some of these questions seem fairly interesting."

Nels shut his eyes and gritted his teeth. Two months of this kind of merry sunshine? It was more than he could

23

take. Maybe he could talk some joker into trading bunks with him.

"All right, now, you got your cruise journal instructions, you got your loose-leaf notebooks to write your journal assignments in, and you got your first lectures scheduled in a few minutes, so let's put the show on the road. For you all, this ship is a floating classroom and laboratory, and the officers and petty officers who'll be givin' the lectures are your professors, and I want you to pay strict attention. Bulkheading at lectures will not be tolerated. Anybody who makes a practice of goofing off will find himself comin' up before me at mast, and that means demerits and extra duty.

"Hear? Okay. Dismissed."

"What's bulkheading?" a short, pink-faced ROTC third classman asked Nels, interrupting some unpleasant thoughts Nels was having about his own eventual appearance at mast to face Sticky Stickney's charges.

"That means leaning back against the bulkhead, especially with your eyes closed," explained Nels. On a ship there were no walls, floors, or ceilings, but only bulkheads, decks, and overheads.

"Well, come on, let's get forward for that talk on Interior Communications. That ought to be interesting," said Oscar. "Say, isn't it lucky we're in the same group, ol' buddy?"

The ships moved out into the broad Atlantic, the destroyers began to roll over the long swells, and it did not take long for the rolling to make itself felt among the midshipmen.

More and more of them, green of face and clammy of brow, found it necessary to stagger below and hit the pad every chance they had. Quite a few had to spend considerable time hanging over the lee rail. Down in the head assigned to the midshipmen, a sign had been installed over one of the johns: UPCHUCKING ONLY.

Though he had not yet lost anything, Nels's head was aching and his stomach was queasy and he was generally miserable. Noon chow seemed like a physical impossibility as he flopped down in his bunk and closed his eyes. At the moment he didn't mind the idea of dying, if only he could die in peace. But peace was not to be his lot.

"Hey, ol' buddy, what you doing in there?"

He opened his eyes to find Oscar looking down at him like a faithful old horse.

"Listen, you don't want to stay in the pad. You've got to fight this thing," declared Oscar. "Come on, we'll go up on deck where you can get a whiff of fresh air — that's what you got to do, stay on your feet and breathe all the fresh air you can. Criminee, it's like the hold of a slaver down here, with poor devils dying like flies," he said, glancing around at the feeble forms spread out on all sides in the tight, crowded space. "Come on, ol' buddy, let's go topside, and we'll have you dancing a jig in no time. I was just reading the menu for today, too, and chow sounds swell, so you don't want to miss that."

Though the effort cost him dearly, Nels raised himself

25

up on one elbow and gave Oscar a glare that was intended to demolish him once and for all.

"Listen, tell me just one thing, Tomlinson," he requested. "Why do you find it necessary to be so eternally and nauseatingly cheerful about every little thing?"

Oscar took the outburst unflinchingly, but the horsy look faded. Now his eyes were so much those of some gentle old spaniel who had been unjustly reprimanded that Nels was ashamed of himself.

"Say, I probably am pretty hard to take sometimes, at that," declared Oscar, as though standing off and taking an honest look at himself. But at the same time he never seemed to lose sight of the main objective, and he did not do so now. He doggedly renewed the attack, turning Nels's counterattack to his own advantage. "I reckon I could explain how I got that way, though, and I will, soon's we get on deck, so come on."

"Oh, for . . . !" Nels was furious, but still he found himself crawling out of his bunk, slipping his shoes back on, and following Oscar up the companionways to the main deck.

"Breathe deep," urged Oscar. "That's it. Don't that help, now? Well, to answer your question —"

"Oscar, I'm sorry I blew my top. Forget it."

"No, I want to explain. It's important. Matter of fact, I can't rightly explain anything at all, because I don't know why it was that ever since I was knee-high to a short grasshopper I wanted to go to sea. I was born and raised on a farm a thousand miles from anything bigger'n a barnyard

26

puddle, except for a couple of muddy ol' rivers, and *they* weren't too close by. I never even saw the sea till I came to Annapolis. And yet all the time I couldn't think of anything else, and when I came to know there was such a place as Annapolis I was wild to get there. For a long time it didn't look like I had a chance in a million, so when I *did* get my appointment I felt — well, I can't tell you how I felt, except that I haven't got over it *yet*." Squinting into the blazing sunlight of Kansas wheatfields had put crow's feet at the corners of Oscar's eyes. They showed now as he glanced at Nels with shrewd appraisal. "I don't guess you were quite as anxious, or feel anywhere near the same. You a Navy Junior, by any chance?"

Nels was surprised. "Yes. My father's class of '34. But how did you know?"

"I just thought that might be it."

"Well, yes and no. It isn't just that. It's . . . well, I don't like the deal the Navy gave my father, that's all." He debated whether or not to tell Oscar all about it, and about his decision to quit Annapolis when they returned from the cruise, but decided not to. He didn't want Oscar Tomlinson bending his ear, trying to change his mind, for two solid months. "Oh, not that I didn't go through plenty as a Navy Junior. I had to come around to some upperclassman's room almost every night. One *second* classman, even. In fact, he gave me the hardest time of all — a fellow who seemed to have it in for Navy Juniors: a redheaded so-and-so named Cornelius Schultz. Corny Schultz. One time two weeks straight he had me wearing a bib, blinders, and a

27

big sign around my neck that said, I AM A NAVY JUNIOR."

"Well, of course I didn't come in for anything like that, but I had my come-arounds, too. Many's the time they had me buzzing down the halls with my arms out at my sides, imitating a plane coming in for a landing on a flight deck, and once I was the star performer in a cruise-box race."

Even in his weakened condition Nels managed to grin at the thought of any man as tall and gangly as Oscar trying to change his clothes from head to foot while locked in a wooden box three by three by four.

"I like to come out of there with a permanent pretzel shape," said Oscar. "Oh, it was great. And for that matter, I don't mind saying there were times when I got tired of sitting at attention on the first three inches of my chair in the mess hall, and answering a bunch of silly questions with even sillier answers that took a lot of time and trouble to memorize. But now that it's over I can look back on all that bracing and hazing and see there's good reasons for it."

"Not good enough."

"Oh, yes. It teaches a feller to obey an order promptly and unquestioningly. Teaches him to hold his temper while he's doing it. Teaches him not to take everything personally. Yes, it taught us plebes a lot. You watch these Rotsies and you'll see that some things will come a little harder for them because they haven't had that kind of training to the same degree."

"Well, maybe. That Corny Schultz, though . . ." Nels was still brooding over his old tormentor. "I never liked red hair to begin with, but since I met him I hate it. What a wise guy he was! For instance, he found out about how my father named my brother Perry and me after famous admirals, so then he started calling me Lord Nelson. 'Law-awd Nelson,' he'd say, with a phony English accent. And pretty soon all the other guys started calling me that, too. I want to tell you, the first thing I intend to do when I get out is find him and poke him in the nose."

Nels bit his tongue at the slip, but Oscar only laughed, misunderstanding the remark.

"Oh, sure. Shucks, you'll be a couple of admirals by the time you get out, and how would it look for one old retired admiral to go poking another in the nose? Hey, you know something? Your color's better. You don't look so all-fired peaked any more. Come on, let's hit the chow-line."

"Please!"

"Now, look, you got to keep eating. That's the most important thing you can do in fighting this seasickness thing. Don't let your stomach get empty. And don't let it bother you just because you have a little trouble. Remember that Admiral Nelson was always seasick for a while every time he went to sea — but once he got his sea legs, look what hot stuff *he* was. Top grease man every time!"

When the word was passed over the loud-speaker system aboard the *Morton,* the old form, *"Now hear this, now hear this,"* was no longer used. It had been shortened to a simple *"Now . . ."*

29

*"Now turn to, turn to. Continue ship's work."* Or, *"Now sweepers man your brooms and give her a clean sweep-down fore and aft."* Or, *"Now the chief quartermaster lay up to the bridge. . . ."* Such was the form that passing the word over the "squawkboxes" took.

*"Now station special sea detail for highline transfer of photographic team"* was the order that brought the third classmen, seasick or well, on deck for a mule-hauling stint. Only a few, unable to rise at all, had been excused.

A tripod was rigged atop Mount 52, just forward of the bridge; the first division deck force, clad in orange "Mae West" life-jackets, was ready to make fast the heavy line once it had been hauled across from ship to ship. "Mule-hauling," this type of line handling was called.

The *Morton* was making a portside approach on the *Wareham,* sliding alongside steadily and smoothly. When the *Morton* had drawn even and the two ships were moving along, side by side at sixteen knots and less than a hundred feet apart, a man stepped to the rail. He was holding a heaving-line, with a weighted rope ball known as a "monkey fist" attached to the end of it. He whirled the monkey fist, bolo-fashion, and heaved. The line streaked in a high arc across the tossing, fuming patch of sea that lay between the two destroyers. It caught on a lifeline on the *Wareham's* O-1 deck, and men scrambled to reach it before it could become disengaged.

The heaving-line, made of cord, was attached to the messenger — a small Manila line — which was in turn attached to the heavy Manila line that was to be secured to

30

the tripod and carry the bosun's chair. One after another the lines were hauled across from one ship to the other and the highline made fast. A trolley wheel, from which lines ran to each ship, had been slipped onto the highline. When the pipe-frame chair had been secured to the trolley, it was hauled across to the *Wareham* and the first member of the two-man photographic team was seated in it.

Nels and Oscar and the others who were handling the highline took their orders from Bangs, whose role was of vital importance and called for considerable experience. When he said, "Hit it hard!" they would heave in hard on the heavy line, taking it hand-over-hand, passing it from man to man; and when he said, "Slack off!" they would let it out just as quickly. In between these commands there were infinite shadings, down to requests to let in or take out as little as a couple of feet of line.

All this was necessitated, of course, by the fact that both ships were rolling constantly during the highline transfer. If the ships rolled toward each other, the line had to be hauled in smoothly and swiftly, at whatever pace was necessary to keep it level. Failure to do this meant a slack line, and a slack line meant that the chair would take a sharp dip, perhaps even dip into the water — and a dunking at a speed of sixteen knots was not a happy experience for the occupant of the chair. If the ships rolled away from each other, the line had to be let out. Failure to do this could mean a parted line, and possibly serious injury to the highline rider.

Three ships were always involved in any highline transfer. The third ship took up lifeguard station a thousand yards astern of the others. In this instance, the destroyer *Weekes*, flagship of the *Morton's* division, was lifeguard.

The highline was the most practical means by which men, mail, or movies could be transferred from ship to ship without stopping. The principal riders were chaplains, doctors, such sick-bay patients as had to be transferred to the larger ships for special treatment, and occasional specialists who had to cover more than one ship, like the photographer and reporter who made up the photographic team. By far the more frequent use of the highline was for transfer of guard mail (intra-fleet mail) and movies.

"Shucks, now we all got to get slicked up," said Oscar, who apparently felt duty-bound now to gripe a little for Nels's sake.

"I never felt less like having my picture taken," said Nels. The purpose of the photographer's visit was to snap portraits of all the midshipmen aboard for release to home-town newspapers.

*"You* don't? How do you suppose the Fabulous Frankhalter feels about it? I wonder what they'll do about him?"

Poor Frankhalter, a first classman, had already won a nickname because he had been and still was the most fabulously seasick of anyone aboard. The Frankhalter who lay below in a bunk was already little more than a shell of his former sturdy self.

"Frankhalter . . ." mused Nels. "Say, let's go below. This I gotta see."

The Fabulous Frankhalter had been left to the last, in the hope that he might show some sign of life. But at last every other midshipman had struggled into blues for his picture and nearly all had been snapped.

"Get him dressed while I'm finishing up these last few," ordered the photographer. "We'll have to do the best we can."

Nels and Oscar stood by watching while three upper classmen clothed the body.

"First time I've ever seen a feller get dressed horizontal," observed Oscar.

"Okay, put his cap on him and stand him up," said the photographer.

"Are you kidding?"

"H'm. Guess you're right." The rest of the men had been snapped standing by the rail on deck, smiling. Some of the smiles had been pale and puny, but at least they had been smiles. But in the case of Frankhalter, there was no sense in asking for the impossible. "Okay, we'll shoot him sitting. He can make like he's studying. Put a book in his hand and prop him up. Lucky he's in a top bunk."

"Come on, Frankie boy. This'll only take a minute."

A groan indicated that Frankhalter had heard. He allowed himself to be propped up into a lifelike pose, his cap set on his head, and a book thrust into his hands. The photographer squinted through his camera sight.

"Man, oh, man! I'm glad we're not taking these in color; I don't have a green filter. Okay, Frankhalter, it'll look better if you'll open your eyes. Tha-at's it. Now smile."

Frankhalter's game try produced a grimace that made strong men shudder. The shutter clicked, and the body was lowered back to rest.

"A few more like that," complained the photographer, "and I won't be feeling so good myself."

"Hey! The book was upside down!"

"Never mind, it won't show in the papers. Folks back home won't know the difference."

Oscar tapped Nels's arm.

"Incidentally, now do you understand why I was glad to get a top bunk? After all, when men are in this shape, somebody's liable to get caught short. Somebody's liable to lean over the side of his bunk and have to let go. Yes, sir — on a tin can a top bunk's the safest place to be!"

They were mule-hauling again, highlining the photographic team over to the *Lawrence*. When the second man had gone over, a midshipman aboard the *Lawrence* was strapped into the chair.

"Hey, what's going on over there?" Nels wondered.

"We're getting one more man," someone reported. "Some guy that was supposed to be with us and got assigned to the wrong can, or something."

"Hit it!" ordered Bangs, and they began to haul the chair across. Since the passenger was wearing a visored cap rather than the blue-rimmed white sailor's hat the youngsters wore, it was plain he was a first classman. And as he swung nearer, dangling in the chair over the dancing waves, it became clear that there was red hair under the cap. Nels's hands

34

dropped from the line as he stared up at the short, square-built newcomer, who was sitting back in the chair buffing his nails on his life-jacket to show his complete lack of concern over the ride. His bright blue eyes played over the group on deck, looking for familiar faces, and they became the eyes of a diving hawk as they alighted on Nels. The redhead bared his teeth delightedly, and pointed.

"Why, Law-awd Nelson!" he cried. And like a wolf upon the fold, Corny Schultz descended upon the deck of the U.S.S. *Morton*.

# CHAPTER III

"**I**F I GET SICK NOW, Oscar, it won't be from the ship rocking."

"Is he that bad, Nels?"

"Listen, this is all the sneering upperclassmen you ever met rolled into one bundle under a head of ugly red hair. Twenty ships, and they have to pick *this* one to transfer him to!" With a sinking sensation adding to the discomfort of his already queasy stomach, Nels contemplated life aboard a small ship with Corny Schultz around. There was hope of escaping the miseries of seasickness sooner or later, but from the miseries Corny could provide there was no escape at all.

At first, during the rest of that day and the next, Nels saw little of him. Corny's bunk was in the after compartment of the midshipmen's quarters, so Nels was at least spared having the same quarters. The times they saw each other Corny chose to look through him haughtily, and Nels managed to keep his own eyes as blank as stone.

As it happened, Schultz warmed up on somebody else.

36

Nels learned this when he and Oscar joined Bangs on the fo'c'sle after knocking off ship's work, to attend a small informal, extracurricular class.

Besides Oscar and Nels, the class in marlinspike seamanship had attracted a couple of first classmen, Benning and Kelsey. Bangs tossed them each a couple of short lengths of line.

"All right now, I ain't got much time to spend on you squirts, so pay attention. Now first off, remember that on a ship, rope ain't rope, it's line. Some say it's rope as long as it's in the original coil, some say it's cordage, but anyways the minute you start using it it's line. You unlay both *rope* ends for about a foot, like this, but what you're splicing together is two *lines*."

Bangs unlaid the three strands in each rope end. His blunt fingers, when they handled rope, became the fingers of an artist, twisting, shaping, and molding the splice as they worked.

When he had completed a short splice, Bangs paused to jerk his head toward a solitary figure standing at the very forepeak with a boathook in his hands. The lad's blue-rimmed sailor hat identified him as a third classman.

"Say, what's that guy looking for, sharks?"

First Classman Benning snickered.

"No, he's standing mail-buoy watch."

"Mail-buoy watch?"

"Yes. That new guy Corny Schultz — he could make anyone believe anything! It's an old gag at the Academy. The idea is that mail has been dropped for us from a plane, and that guy's standing there watching for the mail buoy to come in sight so he can hook the sack aboard. How he expects to hook it from there with a boathook, I don't know — guess he hasn't thought things through that far yet. Honest, some of these dimwits will believe anything."

"Like you," said Kelsey. "I hear tell you fell for the same gag on your youngster cruise."

"That," said Benning, "is not only a foul canard, it's a crock of bull. . . . The truth is, as I hear it, that they had *you* running all over the ship looking for Charlie Noble," he added, referring to the name given the galley smoke-stack. This, too, was a standard shipboard gag.

"Youngsters," said Bangs. "That's what you call these whiskerless wonders, huh?"

"I have to shave every day," Nels defended himself.

"So do I," said Oscar. "Almost, anyway."

"We call 'em youngsters now," nodded Benning. "But traditionally they don't become full-fledged youngsters un-til they see Chapel Dome when they come back up the bay from their first cruise — their 'youngster cruise,' as it's called."

"That'll be the day," said Nels with feeling. He glanced at the solitary figure up forward. "Mail-buoy watch . . . ! Might know Corny Schultz was behind it," he muttered. It burned him up just to think of some of Schultz's past practical jokes. But then he wished he'd kept his mouth shut, because Kelsey glanced at him and grinned.

"Say, that's right, he's the one that calls you Lord Nelson, isn't he? Were you really named after the admiral?"

"Lord Nelson, huh?" said Bangs. He studied Oscar with a heavy frown. "We oughta pick out a name for the cornball here."

"Not to change the subject . . ." said Oscar, "but going back to mail buoys: they got me on that one at the Academy before I'd been there two months. I had to come around to a feller's room, and he sent me on the double to another feller's room to find out what color mail buoys are now. 'What kind of mail, air mail or special delivery?' says the second feller. Back on the double I go to find out. 'Special delivery.' Back again to report. 'Special delivery,' says I. 'Well, but which ocean, Atlantic or Pacific?' says he, and back I went to find out. Gee, I don't know how many things they thought of to ask about, but I know before I was through my tongue was hanging out down to my belt buckle."

"Well, we had a new white hat aboard here last year and right away somebody sent him to get the key to unlock the stack," Bangs recalled. "First he went to the bridge, and the quartermaster said, 'The exec sent it down to the ship's office.' In the ship's office a yeoman told him, 'Chief Barker just picked it up and took it forward to the chief's quarters.' Wherever he went, they phoned ahead and tipped someone off he was coming. They ran that poor knucklehead's behind off of him before he finally caught on."

When the group broke up for chow, Nels and Oscar knew the short splice and the eye splice, and the tips of their thumbs and forefingers were good and sore from learning.

39

After chow there was Assignment G 3-1 in their cruise journal to take care of — "Gunnery Department Organization and Safety Precautions." At 2000 the usual evening movie was scheduled in the mess hall, but Nels was slated to miss it. The watch bill had him down for the 2000-2400 watch on the bridge.

"What's the movie tonight, Oscar? I hope I'm not missing anything good."

"Don't think you have to worry. It's something called *Gog*. Science-fiction stuff."

"Can't be any worse than that Indian stinker we had last night. I think some of these pictures are made just to palm off on the armed forces."

"Still, when you come to think about it —"

"All right, now, don't start being reasonable again, Oscar."

"Oh, don't get me wrong. I can't see much excuse for some of these movies we get, either. I was just going to say it's kind of remarkable to think they manage to show a different movie every night at all, even mostly old movies. I mean, here we are out in the middle of the Atlantic, and all. I wish they'd get hold of a decent Western, though. Maybe when we refuel in the morning we'll trade movies with the *Caloosahatchee*."

"The whattahoochee?"

"That's the name of the oiler we'll fuel from."

"Where'd they ever get a name like that, I wonder?"

Oscar coughed apologetically.

"Well, as a matter of fact, I understand the Caloosa-

40

hatchee is a river in Florida. Just like battleships are named after states, and cruisers after cities, oilers are named after rivers."

"I suppose you know the name of that other oiler, too."

"Well, yes. It's the *Truckee*. River in Nevada."

Nels shook his head wonderingly. "Oscar, every time I look you seem to be around, and yet somehow you collect all this information. How do you do it?"

"Us Tomlinsons have always been naturally nosy," Oscar replied cheerfully, "and I've sure got the nose to prove it."

The squawkbox indirectly reminded Nels that it was seven-thirty.

"Now lay before the mast all eight-oclock reports. Reports will be taken in the athwartships passage abaft the wardroom."

"Now there's a good salty phrase," Oscar pointed out with pleasure. " 'Athwartships passage abaft the wardroom.' As we'd say back home, 'That-there hallway that runs acrost the boat back of the officers' dining-room.' "

Nels sighed.

"Well, I'm about due for my first watch, and I'm certainly not looking forward to it. Who do you think one of the first classmen is that has the same watch?"

"Let me see, now. Benning? . . . Kelsey? . . . Caswell? . . . Nolan? . . . Jergens? . . . Carbino? . . . Golly, I can't guess."

"I'll give you one last guess."

"Okay. Schultz. Matter of fact, I already noticed it on the

41

watch bill. Well, now, listen: plebe year is over, and if you just do your job and keep to yourself —"

"You don't know Corny Schultz," snorted Nels. "He'll find *some* way to make my life miserable."

At a quarter before the hour, Nels reported to the bridge. The man relieving was always supposed to report ahead of time, so that the man being relieved could pass along any necessary information or instructions before his watch was over.

When Nels reported to the officer of the deck (the OOD) he was asked, "Had any experience with the helm, Crane?"

"No, sir."

The OOD turned to the helmsman. "Rizzo, instruct this man in handling the helm, then let him take over and coach him."

"Aye aye, sir." Rizzo was a short, dark lad with what looked like one continuous eyebrow over both eyes. It gave the illusion of a permanent frown. As he began explaining how to steer, however, he was neither friendly nor unfriendly, but simply businesslike. "Well, handling the wheel is no joke, you're working alla time. A good helmsman, he hardly ever takes his eye off the compass, specially on one of these cans, which is no joke to hold on course, the way they can yaw on you. The 'ficial name for the helmsman is the 'steersman.' So now you know it. So forget it. I been in the Navy three years now; I ain't never heard nobody use the word around here except to tell some new guy that's the word that's supposed to be used. Well, so right now we're on our base course, zero seven nine, and we'll probably stay there this whole watch, but that don't mean you can just hold the rudder amidships and go to sleep. She'll swing on every roll, and you got to keep checking the swing, and not use too much rudder doing it. . . ."

The wheel was a big brass disk with a round rubber rim to grip it by. Under the helmsman's eye, Nels began preparing for his stint in the never-ending battle that went on between the helmsman and the uneasy sea. Meanwhile Corny Schultz had reported and was receiving his instructions from the officer of the deck.

"Our guide is the *Iowa,* there in the center. The closest battleship," said the OOD. The fleet was in a circular screen, with the *Iowa* five thousand yards off the *Morton's* starboard bow. "Bearing, one two eight, range five thousand. Be sure to keep her there."

"Aye aye, sir."

The OOD stuck his head into the pilothouse.

"Mr. Schultz has the conn," he informed the helmsman.

"Aye aye, sir," said Nels, and realized with a sort of detached astonishment that Corny Schultz and he were now charged with the task of keeping a twenty-million-dollar destroyer on course and station.

The squat, stocky redhead paced the bridge with a contented stride, obviously pleased with himself and not at all worried about his ability to handle the job. Regularly he went to the binnacle and sighted for a bearing on the *Iowa.* He took no notice of Nels. And Nels was determined not to give Schultz any reason to notice him; he paid strict attention to his instructor, and began to get the feel of the helm. After a while Rizzo watched him silently, standing off to one side.

Except for the presence of Corny Schultz, it was a pleasant time to be on the bridge. The sky was filled with the red glow of sunset, which tinted the clouds that were gathering with a thousand shades of warm but delicate coloring, and the sea was a deep enameled blue that had amazed Nels when first he saw it. In its great circle the fleet was steaming peacefully through the long swells, which had flattened to a point where even the destroyers were scarcely rolling.

Lulled by the evening calm and by the simplicity of his job, which he felt he had mastered already in spite of what Rizzo had to say about its supposed difficulties, Nels's thoughts took wings and flew on ahead of the ship. Fifty-seven days ahead, to be exact. Fifty-seven more days, and then he would be home and his Navy days would be finished. His father — even his brother, Perry — would have to be satisfied that he had given the Navy and the Academy a full try and found them wanting. A lifetime spent with people like Mr. Faye and Corny Schultz on his neck? Not for him, not in a million years. A lifetime of conforming to a thousand rules and regulations, of doing exactly what the Navy told him? No, there were better things in life than that, and he meant to have them. He wondered what Eloise would think when he told her. Eloise! He was lucky to have a girl like her waiting for him, and he didn't mean to wait forever to marry her, either. . . .

Shattering his reverie, a lazily arrogant voice brought him back to the present with a start.

"Nolan," Schultz was saying in a penetrating tone, "are we carrying out some sort of sinuous course exercises? Are we supposed to be dodging simulated torpedoes?"

"No, there's nothing like that on the schedule for tonight."

"Well, then, why are we twisting back and forth?" Corny's head jerked around and his voice knifed at Nels. "Mind your helm, Law-awd Nelson. I'm trying to get an accurate bearing here."

Corny had caught everybody off base. While Nels let his thoughts ramble, the ship had slipped several degrees off course. And Rizzo had drifted into a conversation with the quartermaster about an entry in the log, and wasn't watching.

"Aye aye, sir," said Nels grimly, and threw himself into a desperate effort to bring the ship back on course at once. But in his hurry, he did everything wrong. He failed to take off rudder soon enough in his swing, failed to allow for the time it takes a ship to answer the wheel, failed to remember everything Rizzo had told him. When he tried to correct his mistakes, the ship yawed all the more. Rizzo cursed as he grabbed for the wheel.

"Outa the way! Lemme —"

The OOD, who had been talking to another officer on the wing of the bridge, stepped inside the pilothouse and spoke with lordly severity.

*"Rizzo! Were you watching that man?"*

Then the bridge trembled as a godlike roar smote their ears.

"WHAT'S GOING ON HERE?"

This was Nels's first encounter with the "Old Man" — the skipper, the captain . . . The master who ruled at sea as an absolute monarch, who held them all in the palm of his hand. It was Nels's first encounter, and one he never forgot. He all but jumped out of his skin, all but left his goose-pimpled epidermis standing there while the rest of him dived overboard.

Commander Arthur J. Penn had two voices, a low, quiet one, and a window-rattling blast. There was nothing in between. He knew how to use both voices for maximum effect.

Nels was not the only one who jumped at the sound of the captain's voice. Everybody on the bridge seemed to leap two feet in the air and come down stiff.

"It's my fault, sir," said the OOD.

"I got it now, sir," puffed Rizzo.

"Sorry, sir," mumbled Nels.

The captain's gaze showered thunderbolts on one and all. He was a trim, fit-looking man with a lean, handsome face, and he had the habit of command imprinted on every movement he made.

"Get this ship on course and keep it there," he snapped. "If these midshipmen can't learn to handle the wheel, take them off it and put somebody else on. But when they take over, I WANT SOMEBODY WATCHING THEM EVERY SECOND!"

Gradually things simmered down on the bridge. Order

was restored. Rizzo got the ship back on course. The captain returned to the wardroom movie he had left between reels. And Nels was ignominiously banished to a phone circuit, changing places with another third classman, who stood ready to take over from Rizzo as soon as the OOD got through chewing Rizzo out.

It was the blackest moment Nels had known on the cruise. Everybody was down on him. Rizzo glared at him. So did the OOD. Even the men not directly involved eyed him as though they would like to toss him off the fantail some dark night. And in the meantime Corny Schultz stood looking on and enjoying himself, untouched by it all.

Nels considered the incident a further example of Navy injustice, with the wrong man taking all the blame. Hadn't Schultz started the whole thing? Nels self-righteously assured himself that such was the case, and felt his naturally hot temper boiling up inside him. Fifty-seven more days of it. Could he possibly hold himself in and endure this existence for that eternity?

# CHAPTER IV

"**O**KAY, reveille for the fueling detail. Let's go, you youngsters," rasped a voice in Nels's ear.

It seemed to him he had come down from the bridge and tumbled into his bunk scarcely two minutes ago. On that first, disastrous watch, midnight had seemed endlessly long in coming. By the time his relief finally appeared he had felt bone-tired. And now, to be waked up almost immediately . . . ! Maybe the messenger had made some mistake. He thrust his wrist-watch arm out into the dim light of the compartment aisle and squinted.

There *was* a mistake! Reveille was supposed to be at 0400 for the fueling detail. His watch showed 0300.

"Hey . . . !" He began a squawk of protest — and then cut it off as he remembered. Time change. They had entered a new time zone and the clocks had been moved ahead an hour. Only four hours of sleep between duties, and now he had even lost one of those! Ah, this Navy, it was for the birds, but really for the birds! It was for the crows and the vultures, that's what it was for.

48

The changing pattern of the lumps in the canvas over-head indicated that Oscar was stirring.

"Hey, Oscar." He poked the canvas. "Let's go."

"I heard the man."

Nels slipped out of his bunk and struggled into his pants. The ship was rolling more than enough to make this an acrobatic feat. And the instant his feet touched the deck he found that his queasiness was still there, making things un-pleasant in the pit of his stomach.

"Great day for refueling," he growled.

"You should kick," snorted a first classman who was just climbing back into the pad after undressing. "Jackson got us navigators up to shoot the stars, and then there weren't any stars." He paused to smile sourly. "In case you guys haven't already guessed it, it's a hairy morning out."

Breakfast was a matter of sliding trays and clattering silverware on a slanting table. At 0515, clad in foul-weather jackets, they hit the deck to find the sky cold and sullen, the sea gray and writhing, and the weather deck awash. Nels had scarcely stepped outside for a look, while a more prudent Oscar poked his head out behind him, be-fore the *Morton* stuck her bows under a wave and tossed a foaming flood back along the deck. It soaked Nels to the knees before he could get out of the way.

"When will I learn?" he complained.

"You've learned," observed Oscar.

Alongside, to port, the *Caloosahatchee* wallowed through the tossing seas — a fat, substantial ship with round con-tours and high sides, in strong contrast to the lean, low

49

lines of the destroyer that was sliding up alongside her. On her far side, long black fuel hoses had already been swung over to the *Weekes.* Ships could fuel on each side of the oiler simultaneously. Astern of the three ships, a gray ghost in the heavy morning mist, the *Wareham* rode lifeguard.

The bow waves of the oiler and the *Morton,* meeting diagonally in the narrow race of water between the two vessels, added an extra peak to the churning sluice. Spuming waves scaled the high sides of the oiler and fell off almost vertically along the steel plates as she slid forward through the sea. Green water thundered on the fo'c'sle of the destroyer as she buried her nose in a trough.

In short, they had a moderately rough sea to contend with. Moderate, but certainly not anything spectacular.

"Why, this ain't nothing," declared one of the men who were standing by at the forward fueling station. "You should ought to of been with us coming back from the Med this winter. Fifty-four-degree rolls, we took. Try hanging on sometime when she's rolling fifty-four degrees!"

Lines were fired across fore and aft by men using what looked like toy shotguns, and soon the distance line was in place, with its series of square flags, spaced twenty feet apart, marking the distance between the two vessels. An S/P telephone line, carried across on the distance line, was also quickly hooked up. Heavy lines to support the fuel hoses were secured between the ships. The hoses, swung high in the air on block and tackle suspended from booms, hung in great sagging loops like huge, limp blacksnakes.

"Hit it!"

The black bights began to lengthen out and stretch toward the destroyer, jerking across beneath the highline as the men hauled the hose across. Hands reached out for the heavy, brass-fitted mouth of the hose, wrestled it in over the rail, thrust it into the intake, uncapped it, and lashed it into place. Burlap strips were stuffed around it to prevent any splashing of oil — a good fueling team took pride in doing the job without getting a drop of oil on the deck — and the oiler was signaled to start pumping. Only then was it possible to stand back, relax for a moment, and look aft to see how the men at the *Morton's* after fueling station were doing.

"They ain't even started pumping yet," one of the forward station crew observed with scornful satisfaction.

On the bridge, the OOD stood by the binnacle keeping a constant check on the ship's course, and watching closely the set of the lines to make sure the *Morton* stayed in exactly the same relative position alongside the oiler.

"Come left to zero seven eight," he ordered, to check a slight widening of the span between the ships. They were a little under a hundred feet apart.

"Left to zero seven eight," responded the helmsman.

"Add one."

"Add one," echoed the lee helmsman, and added one turn to the one hundred fifty-three showing on the RPM indicator.

Slowly the angle of the lines between the ships changed, showing that the *Morton* had moved up a trifle. A moment later it was still moving up, and had to be slowed again.

51

"Drop two turns."

"Drop two turns. Aye aye, sir."

Keeping a destroyer in exactly the same relative position in a choppy sea called for considerable finesse. It was seldom that the changes ordered exceeded one or two degrees as to course, or a single revolution per minute — at most two — as to speed. When one turned the ship's bow in, to close the distance, he had to remember that he was, at the same time, swinging his stern away. With lines fore and aft to think about, these swings had to be held to a minimum.

When the *Morton's* fuel tanks were full, the oiler stopped pumping and gave the hoses a blowdown to clear them. This done, they were capped, swung over the side, and hauled back to the oiler. When all lines were clear, the destroyer picked up speed and broke away, easing off to starboard and then making a full turn back to take up lifeguard station so that the *Wareham* could pull ahead and fuel.

Slipping and sliding on a deck made soapy-slick by spray and mist, the youngsters had put in thirty-five minutes of mule-hauling on the wet, heavy lines. By the time the ship broke away it was 0600 and the day's activities had officially begun. Plenty of work was found to fill in the middies' time until their first lectures began. There were lines to be faked down on deck, lines to be coiled, lines to be hung up, and, as always, rain or shine, paint to be chipped.

Not everyone felt that work was in order so early in the morning, however.

On the O-1 deck, just aft of the signal bridge, was a squared-off space filled with crates and sacks of potatoes and covered with tarpaulins. This was known as the "spud locker." It was the best place a destroyer had to store its potatoes. Later on, when spray and sea air had gotten in their work and potatoes were beginning to rot, this space would give off a smell peculiar to destroyers with spud lockers on deck.

For the moment, however, it was a pleasant, secluded spot, with enough extra room under the tarps to house comfortably Kincaid and Marston, two third classmen in search of quiet relaxation. The only trouble with it was that officers like Mr. Jackson, who had taken midshipmen cruises themselves in the not too distant past, knew all about spud lockers. Nels happened to be passing by just as Mr. Jackson was rooting Kincaid and Marston out of their hiding place.

Their sheepish faces drew a lofty snort of disgust from Nels. The idea of choosing so obvious a place to goof off in appalled him. It was kid stuff. It made his skin crawl just to think how foolish he would have felt to be caught there.

The usual routine of lectures was soon interrupted that morning. The midshipmen were assembled on deck to watch the first actual firing practice.

Under dull gray skies still filled with mist, the ships drew up in a long column, five hundred yards apart. A mile and a half astern of the *Morton,* the two battleships had taken their place in line. Visibility was so poor that only one or

53

two ships beyond the battleships could be seen by Nels and Oscar and the others as they stood by the rail on the O-1 deck.

"Take some and stuff it in your ears, you all," ordered Mr. Jackson, circulating among them with a large wad of cotton. "You'll be glad you did when our fives start poppin' off. I don't want any earaches around here except the ones I give you myself."

They obediently stuffed cotton in their ears and stood waiting.

"I understand the battleships are going to fire their sixteen-inchers," said Oscar. "They say they aren't as hard on your ears as the fives — being they're so big, you don't get a sharp crack from them like you do from the fives and threes we've got. Know what a feller told me? He said that every time they fired one of those sixteen-inchers it was just like they'd fired a Cadillac out of the muzzle. That's how much the shells cost."

"Sure, but they give you a faster ride than a Cadillac."

"I guess they could, at that. Ever see one of those sixteen-inch guns up close? Tremendous! They say those barrels are only good for about a hundred rounds before they need relining, and I don't wonder."

Oscar was suddenly impressed all over again with his own figures.

"Say, do you realize what the United States Government is *spending* on us here, just to give us midshipmen this trip and this training? Why, there's millions of dollars in food and fuel involved, and millions in ammunition, and a fleet of ships worth hundreds of millions of dollars —"

"All for little old me," said Nels. "Well, I wish they'd saved their money."

"Oh, who knows? Maybe you'll be a good investment. Heck, what's a few million dollars to a hundred and sixty million Americans if it buys 'em another Nimitz? Or an American Nelson?"

Before Nels could reply to this, the firing commenced, and the spectacle made both of them forget everything else. From the sides of the gray ships rolling under gray skies on a gray ocean, yellow tongues of flame began to dart out into the mist. After an interval the crack of five-inch guns, subdued by the misty air and the distance, reached their ears. Longer tongues of flame leaped from the battleships, and the flat thunder of the mighty sixteens mingled with the crack of the fives. Then flames and roar were close at hand and the deck shook beneath their feet as the *Morton's* guns opened up.

Oscar, as usual, was enjoying himself thoroughly.

"What a show! Say, do you realize most people never get to see a sight like this in their whole lives?" he pointed out.

Actually the same thought had occurred to Nels, but the difference between the two men was that Nels wouldn't have admitted it, much less have mentioned it out loud. He would much rather have given the impression that the whole thing left him yawning. If he enjoyed the show, he enjoyed it grudgingly.

His general glumness did not escape Oscar's notice.

"Still teed off about last night, huh? Listen, exactly what did happen up there?"

"I suppose you've heard talk about it," said Nels bitterly.

"Someone was saying something, yes. What happened?"

Nels described his first trick at the wheel. And as he told the story his resentment poured out, resentment against Corny Schultz, Rizzo, the OOD, and the world.

Oscar listened with close attention, his long face as sympathetic as an elderly family doctor's, and yet having in its expression something of a family doctor's underlying reservations, too.

"Sounds like you were a much-persecuted man," he said when Nels had finished. There was a note of mockery in his words that brought Nels up short.

"Schultz got away with murder as usual, if that's what you mean," he retorted.

"Well, now, your story is all right as far as it goes, Nels, but it does seem to me there's one side of it you've passed over kind of lightly."

"And what's that?"

"The root of all your evils."

"What do you mean? I told you that Schultz —"

"Schultz nothing! The fundamental reason it all happened and everybody jumped on you is because you weren't paying attention to doing your job right. Isn't that so?"

"Why — why —"

"Doggonit, Nels, you must have been woolgathering, to get that far off course to begin with. If you'd been paying attention, and had found you weren't able to hold

56

her on course because you didn't know the job well enough, yet, you'd have told Rizzo right away to come give you a hand and explain what you'd done wrong. So that makes me figure that you weren't quite doing the job the way you should have been, and therefore —"

It was right on the button, of course — everything Oscar said; and nothing can be more maddening sometimes than hearing unwelcome truths. Nels was stung into a sarcastic reply.

"You ought to be a detective, Oscar. Or a chaplain's assistant," he suggested, and turned away on his heel.

"Hey, let's hit the chowline —"

"Be my guest," Nels snapped over his shoulder. "I have other plans."

He was fed up with Oscar, fed up with everybody. And he was so tired he was ready to drop. All he wanted to do was hit the pad for a few minutes while he had the chance.

Nothing ever seemed to work out right for him, though. When he went below, it was to find that Corny Schultz was visiting someone in the forward compartment. He heard Schultz's voice just in time, before he started down the ladder. Rather than go below when the redhead was there, Nels muttered a few things under his breath and trudged back on deck.

The chowline was long and stationary. Eventually word came back that the scullery had broken down. The line would be held up for a while. Nels leaned against the bulkhead and relaxed. All he wanted to do was get chow out of the way and hit the pad. In the past thirty-two hours he had

had but three hours' sleep. During the other twenty-nine hours he had been constantly on the go.

There was one compensation, at least: Oscar was out of sight, up somewhere toward the head of the long line. Nels was glad to be able to rest quietly without having to listen to any more cracker-barrel philosophizing.

The sea had moderated a bit, so that the ship was no longer rolling so much. Nels closed his eyes and thought about home. His father was probably wondering how he was doing, and pinning his hopes on the cruise to make a Navy man out of him. Probably thinking about it a lot — too bad he didn't have Mother any longer to talk to — and maybe writing Perry a letter about it. It suddenly struck Nels that it must have been a lonely year for his father. A lonely year, living alone in the trim white house in the suburbs, limping to the railroad station every morning — he always walked, in spite of the limp; wouldn't leave the car to stand in the open parking lot all day — and returning at night to the empty house. Dad liked his troubleshooting job with the steamship company, and he had a lot of friends; but nothing could take Mother's place, and now he didn't even have a son around to keep him company. Well, he had brought that on himself. Nels had wanted to go to some college close to home, so they could still be together a lot — particularly after they had lost his mother so suddenly, so unexpectedly — but no, it had to be Annapolis. And now, Dad was in for one more blow. It hurt to disappoint him, but at the same time a fellow only had one life to lead, and he couldn't spend it doing something he

58

hated just to satisfy someone else. Not even when that someone was his father. Nels's mind was made up. All he wanted
to do was to finish school at some sensible college, get a
good job in New York, make big money, marry Eloise,
and . . . and . . .

"Crane!"

Nels struggled awake to find Mr. Faye's face swimming
before his eyes. As he brought the ensign into focus, he
realized he had done what he had always supposed was impossible: he had gone soundly to sleep standing on his
feet. The chowline had disappeared.

"Yes, sir?"

"What kind of head covering is *that* supposed to be?"

Nels touched his hat. Instead of cloth, he felt paper. He
pulled it off. It was a triangular paper hat, and on it was
lettered, LORD NELSON.

It was Mr. Faye who was having trouble keeping his face
straight this time.

"Hardly regulation, Crane. I suggest you go below and
try to do better next time."

"Aye aye, sir."

Nels's eyes were blazing as he turned away and dived
through a door for cover. No one, midshipman or enlisted man or officer, was permitted to appear on deck without the proper head covering. Nels hurried below through
the mess hall and down to his living compartment to get
his spare sailor hat. Where had Corny put his hat? His
fists clenched at the thought of Mr. Wise Guy, and again
he counted the days. Fifty-six days, it was now. Fifty-six,

59

and then he'd locate Corny Schultz if he had to turn Annapolis upside down to do it. And when he did . . .

A slip of paper was tucked under the pillow on his bunk: *Your hat was found by a friend and placed in the spud locker for safekeeping.*

It was signed, A. FRIEND.

Nels didn't stop for his extra hat. He stormed back through the empty mess hall and up two ladders to the passageway that ran past Combat Intelligence Center and the radio room and opened onto the O-1 deck. Just outside was the spud locker.

As he stepped out, Nels caught a flash of red hair. It came from the back of an officer's head, an officer he already knew to be Lieutenant (jg) Dennis O'Leary, the ship's supply officer. And facing Mr. O'Leary was Corny Schultz. They were having a conversation. Nels hoped it was an interesting one, interesting enough to keep Corny from noticing him. He didn't want the so-and-so to see him and guess where he was heading. He didn't want to give him that satisfaction.

Four or five quick strides and Nels was under the tarpaulin. Thrust between two potato sacks was his hat. He jerked it out, jammed it on his head, and sat down on a sack to get control of his fury.

Temper had always been a problem with Nels, and nobody had a worse effect on it than Schultz. Only through a major effort did he manage finally to calm down, and to resolve not to give the slightest indication that a stupid practical joke had been pulled on him. After all, the only way he could partly spoil Schultz's fun would be by *not* getting riled up.

As he simmered down, it presently occurred to Nels that he was quite comfortable, more so than he had been all day. It was pleasant in the spud locker, under the tarpaulin amongst the potatoes, and — he suddenly realized — what was more, it now was undoubtedly safe. After all, only a few hours ago Mr. Jackson had caught two men in the spud locker, and he had let all the midshipmen know about it. The last thing he would expect would be that anyone would have the audacity to goof off in there again that very day! Yes, come to think of it, the place was safe as a church for the time being, and now that he was there he was almost tempted to take advantage of the fact. He was still dead-tired. The thought of taking a nap sitting down instead of standing up was so appealing that he had to struggle hard not to give in. He laid his head back against a sack of potatoes, which received it maternally, and closed his eyes to think things over.

"You!"

Nels's eyes flew open and he saw red. He saw, in fact, red hair. It belonged to Mr. O'Leary, and so did the intolerant mouth, and so did the belligerent eyes that looked at the world with a steady sense of outrage.

"This is not the midshipmen's lounge, Crane. Report to your executive officer and tell him I said so."

"Aye aye, sir," mumbled Nels, and scrambled out miserably into the hard light of day. To be caught in the very

61

situation he had felt so superior to only that morning was intolerable — but his shame quickly gave way to wild, pinwheeling anger as he put two and two together. Schultz. Schultz had seen him heading for the spud locker, and Schultz had been talking to Mr. O'Leary at the time.

Nels stalked around the corner of the nav shack with his fists clenched rigidly at his sides. Schultz's other stunts were one thing, but it was going too far when he ratted on a man by fingering him for an officer. Every midshipman aboard would agree with Nels there.

Corny Schultz was standing with a group of first classmen outside the nav shack. Nels saw the redhead through a red mist of fury as he slowly approached him.

"Schultz, that was a rotten lowdown trick."

Corny looked at him as though amazed.

"What trick, Crane?"

"Putting O'Leary on my tail. Why don't you do your own dirty work?"

"Who put O'Leary on your tail? I don't know what you're talking about."

"Don't lie. You sent him to the spud locker. You were just talking to him—"

Schultz had a temper, too. It flared now.

"Don't call me a liar, you cheesy punk!" He surged forward, fists hard at his sides, chest out, a fighting cock aroused.

"Here, now!"

"Hold on!"

Their chests were all but touching as the other midshipmen moved in to get between them and haul them apart. Neither had lifted a hand as yet, but their arms were trembling from the effort of restraining themselves.

Mr. Jackson had been giving the men in the nav shack a little pep talk about shooting better sunlines. Hearing the commotion, he glanced out.

"All right, you fellows, let's not have any football practice — Hey!" His tone changed as he realized that what was taking place was no ordinary roughhousing. He strode swiftly to the group. " 'Ten*shun!* What's all this about?"

He examined the group of men who stood before him at attention. The rapid breathing and purple faces of two of them told him all he needed to know.

"Crane. Schultz. I want to see you in the after wardroom. Wait on deck outside till I get there."

"Aye aye, sir." The words came thickly from both of them. They turned, avoiding each other elaborately, and each made his way below to the main deck.

# CHAPTER V

**T**HEY STOOD WELL APART at the rail, each staring with smoldering eyes straight out to sea.

"All right, you two." Mr. Jackson appeared at the open hatchway that led to the after wardroom. They turned, and Nels followed the upperclassman inside. The officer had seated himself behind a desk. The desk and a few straight chairs, and an overstuffed sofa upholstered in shiny red plastic, were the major furnishings of the room. Adjacent to it were the after officers' quarters.

The two midshipmen stepped into the room, uncovered, and stood stiffly at attention, eyes straight ahead. Mr. Jackson left them that way. The set of his jaw boded no good for either of them.

"I've been checkin' on what went on up there, and I think I've pretty well got the picture. Naturally nobody wanted to say much, but they didn't have to. Apparently there's bad blood between you two that goes back to the Academy."

His eyes swung to Nels's immobile face.

64

"Mr. Crane, you'll be interested to know I also checked with Mr. O'Leary. He assures me that Mr. Schultz had nothing to do with his lookin' in the spud locker. He's the supply officer, so he checks the spud locker often."

"Sir, I was wrong in suggesting that Mr. Schultz was not telling the truth. I regretted it immediately," Nels admitted. "I intend to apologize to him for that. I let my temper get the best of me."

"I quite agree with you, Mr. Crane," snapped Mr. Jackson. "You have quite a temper, don't you? A temper, and also a fondness for not working too hard. You haven't made much of a showing so far on this cruise, but still I hadn't figured you for the kind who'd pick an obvious place like the spud locker to goof off in."

To Nels's surprise, Schultz spoke up at once.

"Sir, he went there looking for his hat."

"His hat? What was it doing there?"

"I put it there, sir."

"Oh, you put it there, did you?"

"Yes, sir."

"You're quite a lover of the practical joke, aren't you, Mr. Schultz?"

The redhead flushed ever so slightly.

"Yes, sir."

"You spend a lot of time thinking them up, I gather. Apparently you have extra time on your hands, and need something better to do. We'll certainly have to remedy that." The lieutenant's eyes bored steadily into Corny's face for several seconds, then returned to Nels. "Mr. Crane, maybe you went there for your hat, but Mr. O'Leary says he found you asleep."

"I had my eyes shut, sir. I wasn't asleep."

"But if Mr. O'Leary hadn't been so thoughtless as to disturb you, you might have been asleep in another minute or so, right?"

"It's possible, sir."

"Why did you stay in there? If you were after your hat, why didn't you just grab it and git?"

"No excuse, sir."

For a long moment Mr. Jackson subjected Nels's face to the same kind of hard, unblinking scrutiny he had given Corny's. Then he sat back and lectured them collectively.

"Gentlemen — and I'd appreciate it if hereafter you'd remember that's what you're supposed to be — I will not tolerate any fightin' between midshipmen on this cruise, and most particularly between first and third classmen. And by that I mean on or off the ship. I had better not hear of any fightin' ashore in Europe. On our visits to foreign ports, you all will be representin' the United States in a military uniform, and you'll be expected to keep that fact in mind at all times. At *all* times. A fist fight between midshipmen could well become welcome grist for the propaganda mill behind the Iron Curtain. So I'm warnin' you now, once and for all: if either of you shows up back at this ship with a marked-up face or any other sign there's been a fight, it'll be the last time you ever fight as midshipmen. I'll fry you right out of the Academy."

He allowed time for the full implications of this to sink

66

in. The two midshipmen stood side by side like statues, eyes front. Nothing in his graven expression betrayed the butterflies that had stirred in Nels's stomach at the thought of dismissal. He wanted to leave the Academy, but he wanted to do so under his own power, not in a manner that would disgrace his father.

"Now, the way I look at it, you seem to need a little extra responsibility, Mr. Schultz. And you seem to need a touch more discipline, Mr. Crane. So in order to take care of that, I am here and now placing you directly under Mr. Schultz for instruction and guidance. You are to report to him each morning and evening, keep him informed as to your activities and progress, and act on any suggestions he may have as to your general improvement. In port you will clear all liberties with him. And as for you, Mr. Schultz, you will be responsible for seein' that Mr. Crane's grades and progress are satisfactory, that he conducts himself properly and stays out of trouble both aboard and ashore."

He paused and glared at them, waiting for their "Aye aye, sirs." These came forth feebly. It was a bitter pill for both men to swallow, this business of being forcibly yoked together.

At last Mr. Jackson nodded.

"All right. You will appear at mast later, Mr. Crane, for unauthorized absence from a study period. And as for you, Mr. Schultz, I'd advise fewer practical jokes, or you may find yourself putting in an appearance there, too."

"Aye aye, sir."

"That's all. Dismissed."

They covered, saluted, and left. Outside on deck, Nels promptly discharged his first unpleasant obligation.

"Mr. Schultz, I apologize for that crack I made about lying."

Schultz glanced back at the open hatchway they had come through. He jerked his head at Nels and walked aft. Nels followed wondering what his intentions were.

The after deck of the *Morton* was deserted at that moment. When they reached it, Corny turned and faced Nels.

"All right, Crane. I accept your apology, because there isn't much else I *can* do under the present circumstances. But that doesn't mean we can't find a quiet place somewhere after we get back from the cruise."

He stared at Nels, his eyes cold with dislike. Square, stocky, barrel-chested, Corny Schultz made a formidable opponent. Nels nodded.

"That will suit me fine."

"Good. We'll have thirty days' leave when we get back. We'll take care of this as soon as we're officially on leave."

"Right."

"In the meantime, we'll carry out orders. Believe me, mister, you're going to get on the ball. If you had any idea of being low grease man, forget it. Report to me tonight after the movies. You'll find me in the nav shack."

"Aye aye, sir." Nels's smart salute made Corny glance around uncomfortably as he returned it.

"And cut out the salutes. I'm going to feel silly enough as it is, having to play nursemaid to you!"

A long panel of light fell across the dark deck from the open door of the nav shack as Nels approached it that evening. The skies were cloudy and the night was black, but the seas had moderated still further, so that their passage had become comparatively smooth.

Nels was going to the appointed spot with all the eagerness of a man about to visit an unsympathetic dentist. There had been buzzing enough all afternoon and evening about the flare-up between Schultz and himself, and much comment on Mr. Jackson's orders. It was bad enough to have to report to Schultz, but to have to do it in front of others set his teeth on edge.

The nav shack was filling up again, now that the showing of the evening movie in the general mess had finished. He saw Schultz's red head bent over a star finder at the high table inside the shack, and when he reached the door and braced himself to report, Schultz glanced around.

"Midshipman Crane, third class, sir," Nels said in a small voice, while some of the upperclassmen present eyed him and grinned.

"Be with you in a minute, Crane. Wait outside," snapped Schultz, becoming a trifle red-eared himself. Nels faded away gratefully into the darkness.

Schultz put on his black-visored khaki-colored cap and came outside. They stood by the rail, alongside the twin three-inch gun barrels of Mount 31. Nels reported on what lectures he had attended, and what work he had done on his cruise journal.

"Okay. But have that Abandon Ship Equipment assignment ready to hand in by tomorrow night. I'll check it over then. And another thing —"

"*Psst!*"

From the main deck directly below them came an urgent signal. By the light of an open hatchway they could see a man looking up at them. The oil-stained dungarees and his bare head marked him for one of the Black Gang — a "snipe," as the men in the engineering section were called. Snipes did not wear their hats below in the engine room and fire room, and sometimes came up and stepped out for a whiff of cool fresh air without stopping to don regulation headgear.

"Catch!" the man whispered, and slung a large, light rectangle of metal up to them in a desperate effort. Corny plucked it neatly out of space and drew back from the rail to see what it was he had caught.

It was a cake pan. A cake pan such as was used in the general mess. Corny and Nels stared at each other in amazement.

Before either could say anything, Mr. O'Leary entered the scene below. Obviously, it had been the knowledge that this watchdog of the ship was approaching along the deck that had spurred the snipe into frantic action.

"Evening, sir."

"Farnum, what were you doing just now?"

"Me, sir? Why, nothing. I just came up for a breath of air, sir."

"I thought I saw you start to throw something over the rail."

"Me, sir?"

"Stop saying 'Me, sir?' I'm not talking to anyone else."

"Yes, sir. Oh — now I know. You're quite right, sir — in fact, I *did* throw something over the rail. An empty cigarette pack."

"H'm. Funny, I thought you had something large in your hand. Like, for instance, a cake pan."

"A cake pan? Sir, I'm a machinist's mate, not a cook."

"Ha. Farnum, don't play games with me. Somebody stole a whole sheet of cake out of the galley, and I intend to find out who did it."

"Well, gee, sir, I'm afraid I can't help you. I have no idea who took it."

"Ha. We'll see. You stay right here. I'm going down to the engine room. If you dropped that pan back down to someone below there, I'll find it if I have to tear the boilers out to do it."

"Aye aye, sir."

Mr. O'Leary stepped inside. Corny and Nels exchanged another wide-eyed glance. Farnum watched until Mr. O'Leary had gone down the ladder into the engine room, and then called up to them in a whisper.

"Hey! You still up there?"

"Yes!" They crouched down for a whispered conference with the man below. "What's going on?"

"Somebody swiped a fresh cake out of the galley, and O'Leary must have heard about it and started sniffin' on the trail. Thanks for saving my neck, pal! I didn't know *where* to get rid of that thing. Just as I was going to chuck

71

it over the side I saw him coming. Hell's bells, I didn't swipe the cake, I only volunteered to get rid of the pan. I'd have been in one sweet mess if O'Leary had caught me with it. Here, gimme it, I'll Deep Six it now."

"No, you can't do that, somebody might hear the splash. Besides, that would be destroying Government property, and I can't countenance that. What's more, I like cake, so I certainly don't want the cooks to be short of cake pans," added Corny, obviously enjoying himself. The situation was exactly to his taste.

"Well, what you gonna do with it, pal? If you stow it anywhere up there and they find it, they'll pin the rap on you middies."

"That's true. Well, the only artistic thing to do with it is to return it to the galley."

"Kee-ripes! You can't do that!"

"Why not?"

"Somebody would catch you sure."

"Oh, I don't know. Let's see. . . . I think I can work it, but I'll need help. . . ."

"I'm your man," said Nels. It was no time to let personalities stand in the way. Corny nodded grudgingly.

"I guess you'll have to be. It'll work best that way. Okay, lay below on the double and fetch a sea bag. Put all your dirty laundry in it for ballast."

Within two minutes Nels was back. Into the bag's roomy depths went the cake pan. They ducked back from the rail and held their breath as Mr. O'Leary reappeared below them.

72

"All right, Farnum. How did you happen to be out here without a hat?"

"I just stepped out for a breath of air, like I said, sir."

"You know you're supposed to wear a hat on deck at all times."

"Yes, sir."

"I'm putting you on report for failing to do so."

"Aye aye, sir."

Mr. O'Leary prowled away.

"Guess he didn't find it," Farnum whispered cheerfully, when it was safe to speak.

"Guess not," agreed Corny. "Okay, here we go."

"Okay. Thanks, you guys. And be careful!"

"Now walk on ahead of me, and if we meet anyone who might be trouble let me do the talking," Corny told Nels. "We'll go below to my compartment."

They went inside and down the ladder that brought them to the passageway abaft the wardroom. Just then the door of that sanctum opened and out stepped the two officers they least desired to see — Mr. O'Leary and Mr. Jackson. Nels's heart bounced like a Ping-pong ball on a concrete floor.

"Well! Are you movin', Schultz?" asked Mr. Jackson, taking note of the sea bag.

"No, sir. I'm establishing a lucky bag for Crane, sir," said Schultz coolly. "If I find anything of his even slightly adrift, in it goes."

"Say, you're really takin' your job seriously, I see," Mr. Jackson remarked. "Do you feel this is fair, Crane?"

73

"Yes, sir," said Nels earnestly. "I can't honestly see any objection."

"Neither can I. Very well, Schultz, carry on."

Even Mr. O'Leary, stern believer in any and all forms of discipline that he was, looked approving. A lucky bag was an old Navy institution. Clothing or other personal articles which were not kept in their proper places — which were "adrift," that is to say — were sometimes placed in a lucky bag. The owner had either to forfeit his possessions or be given extra duty as a penalty for reclaiming them.

The two midshipmen continued on their way, and soon reached Corny's compartment. There a number of middies who were taking their ease and enjoying a bull session chuckled at the sight of them together. Somebody cracked, "There go Martin and Lewis," but otherwise they paid them little attention.

"I've got to hand it to you," Nels muttered as Corny laid the bag gently on his bunk. "That lucky bag bit was a touch of genius."

"Don't think I didn't mean it. Just let me find one article of yours adrift —"

"Okay, okay. Well, what now?"

"That's it, for now. I'll take care of the rest later. They'll be dragging my group out at about 0300 to shoot the morning stars. By then it'll be easy to sneak the pan up and leave it leaning against the galley door."

"Not bad. We can sneak it through the mess hall and up that way. Nobody will be around."

74

"What do you mean, we?"

"Well, you can't safely do it alone. One of us has got to go up ahead and be a lookout, just in case. Come and wake me up when they call you."

"H'm. Listen, the way you've been dropping off to sleep, you probably couldn't make it."

"I'll make it."

"No, I'll get one of the other guys to help."

"Don't. The fewer of us guys involved in this, the better, in case Mr. O'Leary should pick up the trail."

Corny frowned. "Well, that's true," he admitted. "Well, okay. With one of us going first, and the other ready to hand the pan up if all's clear, we can't miss."

"You'll call me, then?"

"Yes, I guess so."

"Good. I'll go first, and —"

"You'll do as you're told. I'm giving the orders."

"Aye aye, sir."

"Okay. That's all for tonight."

Mr. O'Leary was outraged next morning to hear that the missing cake pan, minus the cake, had turned up mysteriously outside the galley door. He demanded that the culprits who had stolen the cake step forward and admit their guilt. He even talked the executive officer into stopping all coffee messes until the villains confessed. In every section of the ship where some sort of hot plate could be rigged, a coffee percolator was to be found. These had provided an endless stream of coffee for coffee breaks.

All over the ship men swore, griped — and grinned. The pleasure of seeing Mr. O'Leary frustrated was almost worth the coffee they were to be denied between meals.

In the meantime, at 0745, Crane made his morning report to Schultz.

"Well, Crane, have you prepared properly for today's work?"

"Yes, sir."

"Going to have that Abandon Ship Equipment assignment ready by tonight?"

"Yes, sir."

"Anything new to report?"

"No, sir. Very quiet night, sir."

"Sleep well?"

"Like a log, sir. Hardly stirred once."

"No trouble with sleepwalking, or anything like that?"

"Oh, no, sir."

"Splendid." Corny eyed him up and down, his hands on his hips. His thick red eyebrows meshed. "Crane, you showed some slight improvement in your general bearing during the past twelve hours, but not so much that it isn't still going to be an exquisite pleasure to punch your face in."

"Yes, sir. Still, I'd hate to see you count on that, sir."

"Time will tell, Crane. Time will tell."

# CHAPTER VI

FOR DAYS ON END the skies remained cloudy. As navigators, the upperclassmen in the Operations and Navigation phase had it easy. There was no sun at noon to shoot, and there were no stars at night.

Nobody in the fleet was able to get a fix, including the ships' navigating officers. Loran (long-range navigation signals transmitted from stations along the Atlantic coast of North America) was already left far behind.

"I like this," Corny Schultz remarked approvingly in the nav shack. "Twenty-one modern warships of the United States Navy, and not one of them knows exactly where we are."

Carbino looked up from a chart of the Azores, which they would soon be skirting, but which were still well out of radar range.

"Mr. Jackson says even the ship's navigator's own estimate probably isn't closer than fifty miles to our actual position. Right now this whole fleet is navigating by dead reckoning, just like Columbus."

Everyone finally had his sea legs, even Frankhalter.

77

Fewer harsh things were being said about life in the Navy, especially about life on a destroyer.

But during their first few days at sea, a large percentage of the midshipmen had been ready to transfer to the Air Force.

"I sure don't know what some of these boys are going to do if we hit any really rough weather," Mr. Jackson had told his assistant one day after a visit to the midshipmen's quarters. "I went below just now to see how many bodies were still in the rack. One of 'em groaned and said to me, 'Mr. Jackson, when's it gonna get smooth?' 'Smooth?' I said. 'Why, man, it *is* smooth! Doggonit, what do you want?' "

In time, however, the seasickness had passed, and life reached a more even keel, even if the destroyer seldom did. The cake episode provided some fun, and the restriction of coffee messes gave everybody something to gripe about for a day or two.

As executive officer, Lieutenant Commander Andrews was second in command aboard the *Morton*. It was he who, to quote the rule book, "has entire charge under the direction of the captain of all matters relating to the personnel, routine, and discipline of the ship," and as he often said, it was the small problems that drove an exec crazy rather than the large ones.

Having ordered the coffee mess restriction by way of backing up Mr. O'Leary's manhunt, Mr. Andrews made a brief speech about it on the fantail to the assembled crew:

"Now, I don't like to cut off your coffee messes, but at

the same time we can't have this kind of pilfering going on aboard the *Morton*. That cake was baked for the whole ship, and it was not fair for a few to enjoy something that was intended for everyone." On all sides, men strove not to grin at these words, and the poor exec, filled with a growing consciousness of how silly the whole affair was becoming, struggled on manfully. "All we want is to know who the guilty parties are and to make sure there'll be no repetition of this sort of thing. If the ones who took the cake will come to me and admit it, we will take no further action on the matter, and it will all be forgotten. But until they do, I'm afraid there's not going to be any coffee for anyone except at mealtimes."

Later that same day the matter was settled. Chief Machinist's Mate Kane informed the exec that *somebody* in the engineering section had taken the cake, and that the whole section was equally guilty, since everybody present in the engine and firerooms had partaken of it. Their identity shielded by their chief, the exact culprits were never revealed. The exec, heartily glad to be rid of this mountainous molehill, permitted coffee to flow again in all parts of the ship, and the cake episode became a part of the ship's history.

Despite a prevalence of poor weather, the sea had its moments of glory. One evening General Quarters was sounded at sunset for a drill that was to include blackout aboard all ships in the fleet. For GQ, Nels's station was on the bridge. Each man aboard had one special and unvarying place to be during GQ, for these were battle stations, and the ship was made ready to fight. Hatches were closed, guns were manned. The main fire control director, CIC, Plot, Sonar — all key spots were staffed for action. The wardroom assumed its fighting role and became the main battle dressing station. Battle ports shielded the deadlights, and the chief medical corpsman waited there with blood plasma, bandages, and other first aid and surgical equipment.

Nature, oblivious to all this practice for war, provided a backdrop of such serenity and peacefulness as comes only at that sunset hour. The calm of evening fell over sky and sea and men alike, as the fleet steamed placidly onward in its great circular screen. Behind a low cloudbank in the west, the sun had set fire to the horizon. Pinned against the broad bank of flaming orange was the black outline of a destroyer above blue water flaked with pink and lavender. For a long time it stayed there, preserving the composition of orange, black, and blue with pastel flecks, an accidental work of art that even the least imaginative man aboard the *Morton* appreciated.

As the sunset colors deepened and faded, the watchers on the *Morton* fell silent, relaxed, and were contented. For the moment it was a privilege to be at sea, to enjoy the robust good health most men found there, and to respond to the quiet beauty of a magnificent evening on the water. A sky of delicate blues and pinks turned to deep blue, deep purple, black. One by one the other ships disappeared into velvet night.

Ordinarily the lights of the ships on the far side of the circular screen, strung out in a flat crescent, gave almost the illusion of a constant seacoast. But now there was nothing. Now it was possible to grasp more readily the vastness of the deep that stretched away for thousands of miles in every direction, breaking on the coasts of four continents.

Each ship was supposed to report any show of light she observed aboard any other ship. "At a time like this, it's good to be among friends," Nels heard Captain Penn remark to the OOD. There was always the green cook who might forget and step out to throw a bucket of slops over the side, or some snipe who might crack open a hatch by mistake.

This time, however, no one slipped up. The *Morton* moved on through the velvet night, a solitary ship on a vast dark ocean, until the signal came to end the blackout, and the great circle of lights began to twinkle again, each set of lights spaced as exactly as though all of them were strung on a cord.

There was, of course, the question of mail.

"Might know it," said Nels. "Last year they had mail deliveries en route by helicopter. But now there's a shortage of 'copters, so they say we won't get any mail till we reach Sweden."

"It's not the helicopters so much as the pilots, I hear," said Oscar. "So many of 'em are busy training new pilots that there aren't enough to go around."

They were sitting in the mess hall after evening chow, writing letters.

"I suppose you're hoping to find a couple of letters from your gal waiting for you, ol' buddy."

"More than a couple, man."

"How many you written her so far?"

"Four. No point in writing too many when I'll mail them all at once anyway. Have you got a girl back home, Oscar?"

"No, not exactly. I'm fancy-free. I'm hoping some little Swedish gal will take pity on me."

"Well, you can have them."

"You mean you don't want to broaden your outlook?"

"Not me," said Nels firmly. "After all, I'm practically engaged to Eloise."

"Practically isn't really. And doggonit, man, you're only nineteen. I wouldn't be in such an all-fired hurry to get roped and hog-tied if I was you."

"That's easy for you to say. You don't happen to be in love with anybody. Besides, Eloise isn't going to even so much as look at another fellow while I'm gone — and I didn't have to make her promise, she said so without my even asking. So I don't feel I can turn around and chase every girl I meet in Europe."

Oscar pursed his lips and looked as solemn as an old horse again.

"No, I guess that's right, not *every* one."

"Not even a few. Not even one," Nels assured him.

"H'm. Well, I'm sure there'll be plenty of interesting ways for you to fill in your time. Trips to museums, visits to the botanical gardens, and so on." And Oscar's whinny deserved richly to be called by its right name: it was a horse laugh.

There was also the question of tours.

From Goteborg, where the ship would remain for a week, they would be able to take a four-day tour to Copenhagen if they had the necessary forty-three dollars and were willing to spend it.

The midshipmen received pay during their stay at the Naval Academy, but most of that pay went toward clothing, gear, and books, with only a modest amount left over for spending money. The Academy considered this amount to be sufficient during the academic year. Financial help from home during that time was frowned on as creating inequalities among the midshipmen. When a man went on his practice cruises, however, extra money was a great boon, and he was welcome to take along any that was offered him by family and friends.

"Forty-three dollars," said Oscar. "Well, I reckon I can swing that. I think I'll sign up. Who knows — maybe some nice little Danish gal might even take more pity on me than those Swedish blondes."

"Oscar, I'm beginning to suspect you of being a cornfed Casanova," declared Nels.

Corny Schultz had something to say on the subject of tours when Nels reported one morning.

"Crane, are you planning to take in Copenhagen?"

"Yes, sir, I thought I would."

"I see. Well, there are two tours. One leaves the day we arrive. The second leaves three days later. I'm taking the first. That leaves you the second. That way I'll get a full week's vacation from you, which should really make my visit to Scandinavia unforgettable."

Even though several of the third classmen, including Oscar, had decided to take the first tour to Copenhagen, and Nels had been planning to do the same, he did not hesitate. A week without Corny Schultz around, in which he would not have to report to him once, was enough to make up for almost anything.

"The second tour will suit me fine, sir."

Corny's fierce, briar-patch eyebrows twitched, and his mouth twisted sarcastically as he acknowledged this announcement.

"I'm overwhelmed to hear it, Crane. Your happiness is my every thought, you know. Dismissed!"

During the morning it was announced that the officer in charge of tour arrangements was ready to make reservations for the Copenhagen tours. When he had a free moment after noon chow, Nels turned in his money and was put down for the second tour.

"Signed up for the tour yet?" asked Oscar, later in the day.

"Yes. But I had to take the second tour."

"The second one? Why?"

"Corny Schultz is taking the first."

"Well, now, look here, he can't rightly —"

"Oh, it suits me. A week of no Schultz — who could ask for anything more?"

"Well, why didn't you say something about it before?"

"I didn't want to ask you or any of the other guys to change your plans. This is my problem."

Before they could discuss the matter any further, the chief boiler technician appeared to lead their group below for a tour of the forward fireroom and a trip inside a boiler that was being repaired — they were in Phase II now, which for them was Engineering. Nels watched his lanky bunkmate start down the long ladder — all elbows and knees; so lean he seemed skinny; and yet a powerful young man who moved with a certain loose-jointed competence and did things remarkably well in an unobtrusive way. In thinking about it, Nels was surprised to discover he had actually been looking forward to Oscar's company ashore. *Well, what do you know? I'm going to miss the old cornball!* he admitted to himself. He suddenly realized how many laughs Oscar had given him, and how he was always wondering what Oscar was going to come up with next.

Disappointment hit him with a rush, and his fist clenched wistfully as he thought about Corny Schultz. Still a spoiler, that Schultz. Still the one who loused things up. Though he had not realized it fully until now, Nels knew that half the fun of the trip to Copenhagen would be gone now that he wasn't going to make it with his own friends, since he was not a person who struck up friendships easily and readily. Besides, practically every midshipman who took the tour would have a buddy or two along from his own ship. Already Nels felt like a loner, an outsider.

Then, too, there was the question of loot.

There were going to be so many tempting things to spend money on in Europe — watches and clocks, cameras and binoculars, silverware and jewelry, Swedish crystal and Danish porcelain, scarves, handkerchiefs, and all the rest of it. Gifts for parents, sisters, and brothers, and for that special girl.

Their supply officer, Mr. O'Leary, was keenly aware of this and had been laying his plans since well before the cruise began. By contracting ahead for a choice selection of foreign merchandise to sell through the ship's store, he would be able to benefit the ship's company in two ways.

First, since the store's mark-up was extremely modest — no more than 15 per cent was permitted by Navy regulations — he would be able to offer outstanding bargains. Second, by channeling as much of the men's shopping money as possible through their own ship's store, he would even preserve for them the best part of that 10 to 15 per cent, since the profits from ships' stores were divided between the ship's recreation fund and the Navy's general recreation fund. The nightly movies, for example, were paid for from this general fund.

As a disciplinarian, Mr. O'Leary had his troubles. Lacking any semblance of tact or finesse, he had managed to make himself thoroughly unpopular everywhere on the ship, from the bosun's locker to the shipfitters' shop. He was disliked by nearly every man on the cruise except for the captain and a few other officers who had insight enough to understand his problems, and patience enough to put up with him. But as supply officer, he was excellent. Alert, scrupulous, intelligent, and tireless, he gave the men excellent chow and a first-rate ship's store.

Among the bargains he had lined up to come aboard in Sweden, it was announced, were several dozen sets of the world's finest cashmere sweaters. There were two sweaters in each set, a pullover and a cardigan, and they would be available at a price which was half to a third of what they would cost at home.

Still, twenty-five dollars was a lot of money.

"Too rich for my blood," declared Oscar. "I don't know any little gal I like that much."

"I guess I ought to forget about it, too," said Nels. "I've already paid out forty-three dollars for the Copenhagen tour, and there's a lot of other things I'd like to buy." Then his eyes softened dreamily. "But still, I can't think of anything Eloise would probably like more. Can't you just see her in a nice yellow cashmere sweater?"

"No, I can't. On account of I've never met her yet."

"Well, you've seen her picture."

"Yes, but I can't tell from that picture exactly how good she'd look in a yellow cashmere sweater." Oscar's long face split into a grin. "I'm only foolin' you. I expect she'd look pretty as all git-out."

"She sure would." Nels sighed. "Well, I don't know. I'll have to think about it. Twenty-five fish! That's a lot of scratch."

# CHAPTER VII

THE ENGLISH CHANNEL was near at hand. Europe was getting close now. And needless to say, Oscar was excited about it.

"Why, I can remember when I thought it was a great thing to go see Higgins Creek after a spring rain, and here I am about to take a look at the English Channel!"

"That's what you think," said Nels. "You'll be lucky if you can see your hand in front of your face, let alone anything more. Do you know what time we're scheduled to be in the Strait of Dover?"

"Well, yes. About 0200."

"Right. That's the United States Navy for you. Brings us three thousand miles to see famous foreign places, and then takes us through the English Channel in the dead of night." Nels was disgusted. And when he looked out at the murky weather and the growing choppiness of the sea, he was also uneasy. "Besides, it's all very well for *you* to talk; you're a good sailor. The main thing I've ever read about the Channel is how it always has half the passengers hanging over the rail on every crossing because it's so rough. I sure hope I won't get queasy again."

Nels had certainly not intended to spend hours on the bridge that night when he didn't even have a watch, but Oscar's enthusiasm for seeing whatever there was to see infected him and kept him there hour after hour as the fleet made its passage through the Channel. The weather remained murky, but the choppiness surprised them by moderating instead of worsening; and in spite of night-time and poor visibility there was still plenty to see.

Even though he knew what an important waterway the Channel was, Nels was still not prepared for the amount of traffic that passed in all directions. A huge luxury liner, bound for America, went by with three decks ablaze with lights. All kinds of freighters and small passenger ships were on the move, both crossing the Channel and passing through it. A string of lights overtook the *Morton* and slid past at what seemed an astonishing speed.

"British corvette," somebody reported.

The quartermaster and the navigator were constantly taking bearings on one lightship after another, and on distant beacons. Lightships, lighthouses, and flashing lights from buoys provided an endless string of channel markers, and all were needed, for the dangers of that narrow strip of water were many, as Nels and Oscar discovered when they studied the navigator's charts.

What maps are to the landsman, charts are to the sea-man. On the landsman's maps the English Channel was a small passageway colored a uniform blue like all the other bodies of water around it. The charts painted a different picture.

Much of the Channel was dangerously shallow, so shallow that in many places the masts of ships sunk there during World War II showed above the water. Many of the buoys they saw marked the locations of these wrecks and of others whose masts lay just below the water. The charts were dotted with them, and with areas where there was still some danger from unexploded mines. Then, too, squarely in the middle there were shoals. Over one long sandbar, mean low water was but one fathom deep — a mere six feet.

Out on the wing of the bridge Captain Penn sat in his chair, watching everything. He seldom sat still for long, but moved about constantly, missing nothing.

"There's one man who won't get any sleep tonight," murmured Nels.

" 'Course not," said Oscar. "You wouldn't catch him leaving the bridge long's there's all this traffic, not to mention the problems of just steaming through the Channel at all."

"Crazy, that's what it is. A man spends years in the Navy working up to where he can be given command of a ship, and then what has he got? A chance to stay up all night and get gray hair from worrying every time anything's doing. Why, he never has an undisturbed night's sleep the whole time he's at sea. Have you read the captain's standing night orders?"

"By golly! Don't tell me *you* have!" exclaimed Oscar, looking pleased.

"Well, I happened to look at them one night. I suppose you've read them, all right — I can't imagine your *not* having read them — so you know he's left orders that every time there's a change of speed or course he's to be notified of it in his sea cabin over the speaking tube. Waked up and told."

"Sure. That's so if there's a sudden emergency and he's called to the bridge in a hurry he won't have to stop and ask questions about our speed and course."

"Well, if you ask me, he has nothing but a lot of head-aches."

Oscar grinned. "Maybe so — but I'll bet you won't turn down a command the first time one's offered to you."

Once again Nels had to restrain himself. The temptation was strong to bowl over this hayseed Navy enthusiast by simply informing him that command of a ship was the last thing he wanted or intended to have. That he had only about forty-three days to go — or was it forty-two? — and then he would be out of the Navy for good. Now, however, Nels had a new reason for holding back. He had grown fond of the big clodhopper, and didn't want to make him unhappy — and he knew Oscar would be stunned to think anybody could feel the way Nels did about the Navy. So Nels held his tongue, and changed the subject.

"What places do you suppose those are?" he asked, pointing to the dark coast of England, some four and a half miles away.

91

Here and there they could see a diffused glow of lights.

"That was Beachy Head, and that must be Hastings," said Oscar, looking up from the chart. He dug Nels in the ribs with an enthusiastic elbow. "Man, do you realize it was right here, back in 1066, that ol' William the Conqueror pulled off his famous D-day? Golly, I never thought I'd ever be this close to the spot!"

"He must have been able to see more than we can, or he'd never have made it," grumbled Nels, peering out into the dark. "Listen, if you think I'm going to stay up half the night to *not* see the White Cliffs of Dover, you're crazy!" he declared. But when the *Morton* reached the strait, shortly before 0200, both boys were still there, peering through the night at shadowy outlines.

With a strong southwest wind chopping at its shallow depths, the North Sea gave them a welcome in keeping with its rough reputation.

For a while the destroyers rolled heavily, and Nels looked with longing eyes across the cold green water to the majestic heavies. The snarling seas snapped at their high sides in vain. They carved a path through the unruly water as though it were a millpond.

After a while, however, he began to think less about the comfort he was missing by not being on one of the larger ships, because this time his stomach remained unaffected. Only a few of the men, such as poor Frankhalter, suffered partial relapses. Not being one of them made a great difference in Nels's outlook. Where a battleship remained aloof, a destroyer became part of the sea, moving with its every move, benefiting or suffering from its every mood. On a destroyer one was truly at sea in an intimate sense that was lost on a battleship, and even in rough weather that sensation of following each movement of the sea could surprise a man into a feeling of exhilaration.

Before long the wind came around to the northeast, the barometer rose rapidly, and the going became easier even though the bitterly cold twenty-five-knot wind was the strongest they had yet experienced. The division commander headed the destroyers straight into the wind, so that they steadied nicely.

"Lots of skunks around today," Oscar remarked as they stood by the rail during an interval between lectures. He pointed to one that was running before the wind a few hundred yards ahead. "Skunk" was the uncomplimentary term given by the Navy to any unidentified vessel it encountered. Each skunk was given a letter identification as soon as it was sighted or appeared on the radar surface search screen (Skunk A, Skunk B, and so on). Its course was carefully plotted, and every effort made to give it as wide a berth as possible.

In the case of the small fishing vessel Oscar had pointed to, the *Morton* turned out of her course to give the tiny stranger plenty of room to cut across her bow. The vessel was a power craft, but because of the strong wind she had staysails set fore and aft. As she bobbed up and down, going almost out of sight when she dropped into a trough, she looked more like two small catboats than a single craft. There was no covered cabin on her, and not a soul in sight on her deck.

"How about that?" said Oscar. "Batten down the hatches and let her run! Set the wheel, lash everything down, and then everybody below stay snug by the stove with a mug of hot coffee! I guess when you fish a sea like this for a living, you get used to taking chances."

Parts of the fleet began to split off to head for their various ports of call. One battleship and a division of destroyers turned north to Oslo. A cruiser and two destroyers steamed south around the tip of Sweden and up to Stockholm. A battleship and two divisions of destroyers followed them through the Skagerrak, and went down the Kattegat to stop at Copenhagen. And the *Macon* and two destroyers, one of them the *Morton,* steamed straight ahead through the Skagerrak for Goteborg, on the western coast of Sweden.

Despite poor weather and rough seas, the destroyers waged their unending fight, almost to the moment of entering the harbor, to belie their "rust bucket" name. Visitors would be allowed aboard in port, and the ships had to look their best. All over the *Morton,* as she neared port, men with paintbrushes stooped, and stretched, and squatted, disregarding the drizzling rain as they slapped a fresh coat of paint on decks and bulkheads, overheads and hatches.

The *Morton's* course was altered to due east, and all

night long she wallowed in a trough, pitching as well as rolling. It was impossible to sleep.

"Craziest feeling I ever had," Nels called up to Oscar as they lay in their bunks. "It's like spiraling through space. I'm describing perfect circles in the air."

"Twenty-foot circles, at that," Oscar pointed out. "This can's bow is rising and falling a good twenty feet on every wave. But hang on, now. Just one more day and then there'll be dry land, some of that smorgasbord stuff they eat, and scads of those pretty blond Swedish gals."

"And mail! Letters from Eloise," Nels added loyally.

Land, undeniable and approaching, looked good to all hands. Fifteen days at sea was a long time, fifteen days of being constantly on the move without stopping once, particularly for men who were not used to it.

The grim, rugged, rocky coast reminded Nels of Maine, where he had once spent a summer. The entrance to the harbor was peppered with small islands, most of them too small to be inhabited. Though it had been a stranger to them for many days, the sun came out that morning and shone brightly on the red roofs of a fishing village's white frame houses, clustered on the shore.

Goteborg's harbor was small, but every inch of it seemed to be in use. Freighters and steamers at pierside and in drydock lined both sides of it, and several ships were under construction in the huge shipyards. Barges, small lumber boats with decks piled high with precisely stacked planks, excursion boats, and ferries scooted about in every direction. In a small naval yard, minesweepers and submarines lay nested alongside a wharf. Goteborg was Sweden's first port, even overshadowing Stockholm.

The crew and midshipmen of the three visiting warships fell into ranks by sections along the decks, as was customary when entering port. Salutes were fired by a shore battery, and returned by the guns of the *Macon*. High on a rocky point, a Swedish naval detachment stood at attention and saluted while its band played "The Star-spangled Banner." Aboard the warships, whistles blew, men snapped to attention, and officers rendered the hand salute. Merchantmen, sliding by on their way to sea, dipped their colors in the time-honored salute to warships.

Two boatloads of Girl Scouts were learning to row in whaleboats, and each girl seemed to be operating independently, to judge from their ragged performance; but suddenly there was order as their oars flashed in the sun, up-ended precisely in a salute. Aboard the *Morton* the boatswain's pipe sounded and the salute was punctiliously returned.

Clean and tidy-looking, Goteborg was for many of the midshipmen the first foreign city they had ever seen. It was a city of buildings ancient and modern, of old churches and fortresses and new apartment buildings, and without seeming strange it was still different in a hundred ways from any American city they knew.

"Well, come on, let's get squared away and ready to go ashore," said Oscar, when the ship reached its mooring and they had gone below to their compartment. "When liberty commences at 1300, I'll be r'arin' to go! I don't mind saying it's going to be good to set my feet on dry land for a change, much as I've enjoyed the trip over."

"But you can't very well go ashore at 1300, Oscar. Your Copenhagen tour group is scheduled to leave the ship at 1500!"

Oscar grew very busy shining his liberty shoes. For a moment he continued to buff their already mirrorlike surfaces. Then he straightened up and glanced at Nels with a wide, sheepish grin.

"Now, look here, ol' buddy, you know how curious I am. Why, I'd be in such a fever of curiosity, wondering how your struggle with temptation here was coming along, that I wouldn't half appreciate Copenhagen. I'd always wonder how you went about resisting beautiful Swedish blondes, and I might never get the straight story of it from you. Another thing, I might want to be true to some little ol' gal myself one of these days — it *could* happen, I suppose — so I better find out how it's done. Well, anyway — so what I did, I went and had myself changed to the second tour."

Nels was almost as dumbfounded as he was pleased. Two weeks ago he had put this fellow down as an ordinary eager beaver, a barnyard pest. Today he heard with deep pleasure that he was to have the man's company ashore. He knew that Oscar might well mean the difference between a dull time and a good one in Copenhagen.

He also recognized Oscar's action for what it was: an act of simple goodness. Oscar could have had as good a time on the first tour as on the second, because he made friends easily and everybody liked him; but he had changed tours because he couldn't leave a buddy in the lurch.

Oscar poked Nels in the ribs. "I hope you don't mind my hanging around, ol' buddy."

Nels poked him back. "Heck no, I don't mind," he said, covering his feelings. He was humbly grateful, and yet it wasn't the sort of thing you could thank a fellow for in so many words. He sat down on his bunk, then sprang up and gave the old cornball a swat on the shoulder. "Why, you might even say I'm practically glad, ol' buddy!"

# CHAPTER VIII

Almost as soon as the *Morton* was moored, small craft began to arrive on various errands. A Swedish naval officer assigned as liaison officer appeared to see the captain, and several salesmen to see the supply officer. As part of Goteborg's welcome, a telephone crew began immediately to run a cable out to the ship to provide ship-to-shore telephone service complete with an English-speaking operator, a young Swedish sailor. Harbor boats puffed alongside with consignments of supplies. A tug appeared towing a wooden float to be secured to the *Morton's* starboard quarter for use as a landing.

The *Morton* was moored to a buoy in the channel, a few hundred yards from a landing pier. At 1300 midshipmen in dress blues and white-covered officers' caps began to go ashore in the *Morton's* motor whaleboat. In the second boatload were Nels and Oscar. As they hurried up the landing and onto the waterfront street, the cement pavement seemed to rise and fall in gentle swells It took them a few minutes to get their land legs.

"According to that telephone operator," said Oscar — of course he had already had a friendly chat with him and picked up considerable information about Goteborg — "if we turn left and follow the waterfront till we come to a street with a canal in the middle of it, and then go up that street, it'll take us straight to the center of town. . . . Say, doesn't it look funny to see all the signs in Swedish? I reckon the only thing that would look funnier is if they weren't."

When they reached the canal, Oscar pulled up short. Balboa discovering the Pacific could scarcely have radiated more satisfaction than did Oscar as he grabbed the camera that was hanging around his long neck.

"My first canal! Got to get a picture of this." But then the angle didn't satisfy him. "Maybe I'll do better from across the street."

Nels started across. The tires of a small car screeched. Just in time, Oscar snatched him back.

"I knew I'd better keep an eye on you. Now, listen, Nels, don't forget this is Sweden, where they drive on the left side instead of the right." They waited while two cyclists went past. "Ever see so many people of all ages on bicycles? Look at that old lady! I've got a grandmother who looks exactly like that, but I'll bet she hasn't hopped on a bike in sixty years."

The broad canal, crossed by handsome stone bridges and flanked by such distinguished old buildings as the Cultural Historical Museum, Kristine Church, and the *Rådhus*, or Town Hall, caused them both to use up considerable film. They rubbernecked through the shopping district, and Nels bought a bud vase for an aunt who had asked him to bring back some Swedish crystal.

They strolled on through the city, reveling in warm sunny weather after so many cold gray days at sea. As they crossed a bridge over another canal, an open sightseeing boat passed beneath them and several children waved. People smiled and nodded to them as they walked along, conspicuous in their uniforms. Goteborg's citizens seemed bent on making them feel welcome. And everywhere they looked they saw the attractive blond girls they had been led to expect. The percentage of blondes was astonishing.

"By golly, two weeks is a long time to go without seeing a tree, a house or a blonde," said Oscar. "It's wonderful just to look at people and kids and green grass again. And blondes."

"Oscar, you're a bad influence," said Nels, and turned his thoughts resolutely toward Eloise. "Say, by the time we get back to the ship there ought to be some mail."

"You really think your gal will write you?"

"I'm not worried."

"Are you going to the dance at the Town Hall tonight?"

"Well, sure, we *have* to go to that. We have orders."

"I understand they've rounded up the cream of the local crop to dance with us. You going to dance?"

"Why not? There's no harm in just dancing, especially when it's your duty as a representative of your country."

"Just so you don't go beyond the call of duty, of course. Come on, let's cross over — here comes another of

101

those excursion boats. I want to get a picture of it, and then let's pick a place and start eating."

Nels automatically glanced to his left and stepped off the curb. He had forgotten again about the direction of traffic. The bicyclist coming from the right did her best to avoid him, but she still skidded into him and came straight at him over the handlebars. Nels staggered back and sat down with his arms full of slender Swedish blonde. Nearby, a tinkle of Swedish crystal indicated that the bud vase had suffered.

For an instant the girl sat on him, fuming as she pulled her skirt down over a long and shapely pair of golden tanned legs. Then she scrambled to her feet and put her hands on her hips, a tall, slim, and furious girl. Even with a scowl on her flushed face she fulfilled every requirement as to looks and figure that any young American tourist could reasonably have asked for. When she spoke, she spoke in English, with an uncompromisingly Swedish accent.

"Why don't you watch out?"

"I'm sorry, I keep forgetting which way to look," Nels said, getting up. "Are you all right?"

She felt her elbows and switched her skirt aside for a look at her knees. They were not only uninjured, but very pretty.

"I suppose so," she said, but her face still remained stormy.

"What about your bike? I'll have it fixed if there's any damage," he assured her, picking it up to examine it.

102

Oscar had retrieved Nels's package. He held it up to his ear and rattled it.

"Ol' buddy, you need a new vase."

"Well, at least the bike seems all right."

"Let me have it, please." She turned up her nose, which was short, straight, and saucy to begin with. "I suppose it will be like this for a whole week in Goteborg, now that you Americans are here."

"What have you got against Americans?"

"I don't like them."

"Why not?"

"They think they own the world."

"What makes you say that? Have you known many Americans?"

"No, but my Cousin Ludvig has, and he's told me all about them. He is in the merchant marine and has visited America many times."

"What part of America?"

"Hoboken."

Nels laughed. "Well, I don't know who he met there or what he saw, but there's a lot more to America than Hoboken."

"I know that, you may be sure. I have studied about America in school. We are forced to."

"Are you forced to learn to speak English so well, too?" asked Nels, grinning. She gave him a scornful look, and the sun flashed on her bright blond curls as her chin lifted.

"That's different. I would like to visit England some day. You know, that is where English is truly spoken," she added as a crusher. "Besides, I will need English when I become a secretary."

"Oh, you're going to be a secretary?"

"Yes. May I have my bicycle now, please."

"Before it's even been checked over to see that it's all right? If there's any damage, I want to pay for it. Isn't there somewhere near here, some bicycle shop, where we can have it checked?"

Nels was amazed at himself. At home he was always tongue-tied around girls he didn't know, especially dazzling ones, yet here he was in Sweden talking right up! Maybe it was because this one was already so mad at him that he could feel he had nothing to lose by being forward. Or maybe it was because he was already practically engaged to Eloise and therefore not worrying so much about what this girl might think of him. Whatever the reason, he was enjoying himself.

"I'm sure it's all right," she said, but before she could take the bike Nels had swung onto the seat and begun pedaling in a circle, waggling the handlebars as he went. "See?" he cried over his shoulder. "Something's bent! This is terrible!"

His sudden clowning surprised a giggle out of the girl.

"Stop that!" she scolded, pulling her face back into a frown. But then she giggled again. "Oh, how silly, an American midshipman on a girl's bicycle!" And she clapped her hands in delight as Oscar's camera snapped.

"I'll give you a print of that one," Oscar assured her

104

genially as he wound his camera. Nels coasted to a stop beside them and beamed at her.

"Listen, you were forced to study America in school, so how about studying a couple of Americans first hand, for a change? Can't we sit down somewhere and talk for a little while?" He pointed down at a two-decked excursion boat that was moored at the bank of the canal. "Isn't that some sort of restaurant?"

"Yes."

"What do they serve?"

"*Konditorei* and coffee, of course."

"*Konditorei?*"

"Pastry. Cake."

"Say! What are we waiting for?" cried Oscar.

"Won't you join us, please, just for a few minutes?" Laughter had softened the girl's anger beyond repair. She looked tempted. She also looked thoroughly gorgeous. If she had been an eyeful even with a frown on her face, she was sensational when she smiled.

"Well, perhaps. There are some things I would like to know about you Americans. But I could only stop for a few minutes."

"Let's go. By the way," said Nels — and strove to trot out his best manners — he was now representing the United States in a big way — "permit me to introduce Midshipman Oscar Tomlinson. . . . And my name is Nelson Crane."

"My name is Kristine Yonson," she replied, and shook hands formally with each of them.

105

They boarded the large white boat and sat at a table on its airy top deck.

"Yonson," said Nels. "How do you spell it?"

"Yee — ooh — hoh — en — ess — ooh — en."

The boys exchanged a blank stare. Nels produced a small notebook.

"You'd better write it."

Kristine wrote out the name.

"Oh! *Johnson!*" said Nels. "Why, that's a common American name."

"Sure, we've got lots of Johnsons in Kansas," said Oscar.

Kristine looked at them indignantly. "Well, where do you think the name *came* from? You see? Just like I say. You Americans think you own the world!"

Both boys leaned back and laughed so heartily that she bit her lip to keep from smiling.

"You're very silly. You think everything is funny," she declared severely. "And also, here my name is not pronounced however you said it — *Johnson* — but like I said it."

"Yonson. Right. Anything you say."

"I can also tell you it's lucky my Cousin Ludvig wasn't with me today. He would have knocked your heads together good. He is big, big, and becomes angry very quick."

"Is your Cousin Ludvig here now?"

"No, he's on his ship."

"Good. Somewhere in the Antarctic, I hope?"

"In Stockholm now, I think."

"Too close. Oh, well . . ."

"You think I am fooling!"

"No, we don't. But let's talk about something pleasant. Let's talk about Sweden and America."

And for an hour they did. By the end of that hour, Cousin Ludvig had lost quite a bit of ground.

"Oh, you make me laugh even when I don't want to," Kristine complained. "Now I know the truth. Americans are not bad, only crazy."

Nels brought up the subject of the dance that was to be held that night at the *Rådhus*.

"I certainly hope you're going to be there."

"I have an invitation, but I had almost made up my mind not to go," said Kristine, throwing out a womanlike hint.

"Almost, huh? Then you will go? That's wonderful. Then I'll go." Nels grinned. "I would have had to go anyway, but I didn't want to very much, until now. Will you be my partner?"

"I'm not sure that can be arranged," said Kristine primly. "We will be introduced to partners by the official hostess, and may not be able to choose."

"We'll work it somehow," said Nels. "That is, if you're willing."

"We will have to see."

"Say, do you have a friend for me?" asked Oscar. "Small and blond, if possible?"

Kristine turned her level blue eyes his way and looked him over thoughtfully.

"Oscar. That is a Swedish name, you know."

"Yes, I know. I came by it natural. I'm part Swede on my mother's side."

"So?" Kristine looked approving. "Good. Even part is some help. Yes, I have a perfect friend for you."

"Small and blond?"

"Yes."

"Swell! About a hundred and fifty-eight centimeters tall," he added. And when Nels looked amazed he explained, "I figured it out the other day, just for use in these centimeter countries."

Kristine was nodding. "I know exactly the girl. And very good-looking, too. I will bring her with me, because she also has an invitation."

"Well, gosh all hemlock, if she's half as pretty as you, I'll be happy," declared the rustic cavalier, and beamed at his friend. "Nels, our evening is made. Come on, let's all have some more pastry."

"No, thank you, I must go," said Kristine, rising. "But maybe something will arrange itself at the dance tonight, and we will see each other then."

When Kristine had ridden away on her bicycle with her full skirt flowing out behind her and her golden hair dancing as it brushed her shoulders, the boys returned to their sightseeing. But Oscar was hard to live with.

"Hot diggety! Not here one hour and you've already got

a blonde sitting on your lap. It sure was instructive to watch the way you went about resisting her."

"Ease off, will you? I was only trying to be nice to her, is all," Nels claimed. "She's a nice girl, and there's certainly no harm in dancing with her. I have to dance with *someone*. If it wasn't her, it would be someone else. And remember what Mr. Jackson said, about how we're representing our country in a semiofficial capacity. We couldn't let her go away thinking bad things about America."

"No, we sure couldn't, now could we?" Oscar smacked his hands together. "Well, I'll be anxious to see this little blondy she's bringing for me."

"A hundred and fifty-eight centimeters!" snorted Nels.

"Kee-rect. That's five feet two, ol' buddy, practically on the nose!"

When they reached the *Rådhus* that night, Oscar suggested to Nels that they hang around outside for a while, instead of going in at once.

"Maybe we can meet the gals out here and make sure of getting together. On deals like this, I don't trust the Navy too far."

"What's this? A word of criticism?" marveled Nels.

"Well, you know. If there's a couple of duds waiting around in there, some officer's liable to grab us and assign us to them by the numbers, and then where'll we be?"

"You're right, Oscar. Let's stay out here."

They stood on the front steps and looked over the girls

who were beginning to arrive. Presently Oscar revised his estimate.

"Nels, I take everything back. I haven't seen a dud yet. And only about four girls so far weren't blondes, have you noticed?"

"Noticed? Listen, I have only one thing to say about what I've seen so far."

"What's that?"

"Wow."

Behind them an officer suddenly appeared in the doorway. He noticed them.

"Men."

"Yes, sir?"

"Inside."

The officers in charge of the affair did not intend to let any midshipmen slip through their fingers if they could help it. They wanted heavy attendance.

Reluctantly, the boys entered. The officer pointed.

"Upstairs."

They marched off up the stairs.

"The Navy!" muttered Nels. "The Navy can put military discipline into anything!"

Goteborg's handsome Town Hall seemed to have been built for just such occasions as the dance. From an impressive first-floor entrance hall, twin marble staircases led up to a balcony, one toward the front, the other toward the rear. The girls, as they arrived, were gathering along the rear of

110

the balcony. The midshipmen were sent up the front staircase.

"Look, there's Kristine!" said Nels. "She was already in here!"

From the cluster of some fifty girls, Kristine waved to them. They waved back eagerly and exchanged a number of unintelligible signals with her before an officer told them to keep moving.

"I wonder which of those gals around her is mine?" said Oscar. "Now, let's watch our step here and not get caught short. See how the system works? They send us through these rooms here, and we'll come out at the other end of the balcony where the gals are. We'll be paired off with them by that lady with the corsage, who's probably the official hostess, and then we'll head for the ballroom. So we've got to jockey for position, and the girls will have to do the same. We can't step out of that room till they've worked toward the front of the bunch."

"Mr. Tomlinson, your tactical analysis of the situation is superb. Lead on."

They walked through the series of formal reception rooms and joined the group of midshipmen who were gradually congesting the room that opened onto the rear of the balcony where the girls were.

Actually the girls had more mobility than the boys. The midshipmen had to step out one by one and were likely to be urged forward by an officer who was standing by if they did not keep the line moving briskly enough. The girls,

111

however, were able to choose their own split-second for stepping forward.

It was a pleasure to watch them work.

"And the Navy thinks it's good at maneuvers!" remarked Oscar as they watched couples being paired off. "Why, the stuff we do is child's play compared to what these gals are pulling off. 'Specially the string beans. I haven't seen a tall gal get stuck with a short feller yet. See 'em talk it over under their breath and pick their fellers? Believe me, I'm glad Kristine brought a friend for me!"

"Look, there's Kristine now."

"I see her. And I'll bet that's my drag on her left there — see that cute little blond trick? Come on, get into position, boy."

"Okay, get behind me."

"Let's go."

As Nels stepped out of the room, Kristine swayed gently into the front and center of the group, murmuring a few words to left and right as she did so — probably the Swedish equivalent of "Lay off, girls, this one's mine." She stepped forward and said good evening to the hostess.

The hostess asked Nels to state his name. She read Kristine's to him from her invitation, and showed it to him.

"Oh — Yonson," said Nels, grinning, and offered her his arm. "Good evening, Miss Yonson."

"Good evening, Mr. Crane."

"You brought your friend for Oscar, I hope?" he asked as they joined the column of couples that was slowly moving into the ballroom.

112

"Oh, yes." She glanced around. "Here they come."

Oscar was falling into line behind them with a flabbergasted look on his face and a tall brunette on his arm.

"Hey!" Nels stared at Kristine. "You said a small blonde!"

"Oh, that one couldn't come."

The innocence in her blue eyes seemed overdone.

"Kristine," said Nels, "I don't think there *was* any small blonde."

The innocence vanished in a gay twinkle.

"Ulle Gustavson is a lovely girl, and she's just right for your friend," she declared firmly. "He's much too tall to waste on a short girl."


Liberty for third classmen ended at 0100. They had to be waiting on the landing by that time.

At 0100, when Nels and Oscar raced onto the landing and joined a large group of waiting midshipmen and white hats, the sky was still light. It was the midsummer time of year when Goteborg had no real night at all. During the next few days, the country a few hundred miles to the north would fulfill its role as the Land of the Midnight Sun, a place where the sun never set.

Looking back on the evening, Oscar had about decided to forgive Kristine for double-crossing him.

"You know, for a tall gal, and a brunette, that Oola is all right," he admitted. "Oola" was the closest he could come to the Swedish pronunciation of Ulle's name. "We have a lot in common, too, her living on a farm, and all. I wonder how Kristine figured out that I was a farm boy my-self, when she doesn't know anything about America?"

Nels laughed and slapped him on the back. "I can't imagine!"

"Well, anyway, she's all right, that Oola. I'll be mighty interested to see her folks' farm when we ride out there tomorrow." They had a date with the girls to bicycle out into the countryside. Oscar's eyes grew quizzical as he looked Nels up and down. "By the way, you sure are being nice to that Kristine."

"I only shook hands with her when we left," Nels pointed out. "I didn't kiss her good night, or anything like that."

"I know — but who was doing the resisting?"

"Listen, you know a girl like that isn't going to let you kiss her the first time you take her out. Why, such an idea hardly entered my mind," Nels claimed feebly. O, Eloise! Why was she so far away, and Kristine so near? It wasn't fair. If only there was mail waiting for them! That would bring Eloise near again, and help him to keep in mind that when all was said and done she was the only one who counted.

Tucked under the blanket on his bunk, Nels found mail. Two letters from his father, and seven from Eloise. Seven long, loving letters, telling how much she missed him. She told him everything she had been doing, and although she did mention playing tennis a couple of times with a fellow named Ronald, it was plain that Ronald was merely some-one who was around, and not a person of any significance.

"What a girl!" said Nels, when he had read the letters

114

all over twice. "Makes me ashamed to think I've even so much as *looked* at another girl. Well, I know what I'm going to do," he declared, getting a noble look on his face that filled Oscar with alarm.

"Not break your date for tomorrow, I hope?"

"Well, no," said Nels. "After all, that wouldn't be fair to the rest of you. I mean, a bargain's a bargain, so to speak. But what I am going to do is — first thing in the morning I'm going to the ship's store and spend twenty-five bucks on a set of those sweaters for Eloise!"

# CHAPTER IX

THE GUSTAVSON FARM was an hour's bicycle ride from the city. Oscar toured every inch of it with Ulle and her father, and although she had to be their interpreter, Mr. Gustavson and Oscar still spoke the same language where farming was concerned. Oscar understood and appreciated everything he saw. He was unquestionably the hit of the season as far as the Gustavsons were concerned.

Late in the afternoon they pedaled back through the lush green midsummer countryside to Goteborg, debating as they went about what they should do that evening.

"We're supposed to go to another dance at the *Rådhus*," said Nels. "Do you want to go again?"

"You don't understand. We had invitations only for the first dance," said Kristine. "There were so many girls wanting to go that we were divided into two groups, one for each night. Some of the girls who went last night are going to change the dates on their invitations and use them again tonight, but I would not want to do such a thing. Besides, the hostess knows me," she added mournfully.

"I think we should go to Liseberg tonight," said Ulle.

"Yes, I think they should see Liseberg."

"That's your amusement park, isn't it?"

"Yes. Next to the Tivoli in Copenhagen, the finest in the world. Isn't it, Ulle?"

"That's what everybody says."

"You know a place in America called Coney Island?" Kristine looked down her nose at Nels. "Well, my Cousin Ludvig went there one time and he says it's ugly and can't be compared to our Liseberg."

For once, Kristine's king-size cousin was right about something. Set among grassy slopes, trees, and banks of flowers, clean and beautiful, Liseberg was unlike any amusement park the boys had seen before.

The park's showpiece was the great concert hall with a large rectangular mirror pool in front of it. The concert hall and the restaurants that bordered the pool were salmon pink in color, with green-and-white trim. Flags waved from the buildings, and everywhere there were flowers, large and vivid.

Outside the hall, in which a symphony concert was scheduled to begin later, a band was playing. Presently, on an outdoor stage at one end of the pool, a troupe of twelve girls appeared and danced. They looked as wholesome as cream, with complexions to match.

All the usual amusement park attractions were present at Liseberg — the roller coaster, merry-go-round, dodgem cars, airplane rides, Ferris wheel, funhouses, and the rest. There were also some surprises.

117

"Hey, look! One-armed bandits!" said Oscar, as they came upon a penny arcade type of concession packed with slot machines. "Why, back home we've only got one state in the Union where these things are legal."

There were also a number of roulette wheels. Gambling was on a modest scale — 25-öre pieces, worth about five cents, were used — but everybody was allowed to play, even children. While they watched, one eight-year-old hit a number and won a handful of coins.

There were many other differences between the ways of Sweden and America, too. For example, it occurred to Nels while they sat drinking beer with their dinner that back home in America he and Oscar, being minors, could not even have been served beer in a public place. Here they could have beer and even hard liquor, such as the fiery *snaps* the Swedes favored. On the other hand, it was illegal for anyone to have anything to drink in public places except with meals.

The crowd at Liseberg contained more than a sprinkling of uniforms. Needless to say, hundreds of the visiting sailors and midshipmen had found their way to the park, some with girls, some looking for girls. Nels and Oscar saw many familiar faces, including that of Goodman, one of the gang in the forward fireroom, who gave them a cordial wave. Ever since the cake episode, Nels's stock had been high among the men of the engineering section, all of whom knew about the part he had played.

The two midshipmen took the girls on the roller coaster, the Ferris wheel, and the airplanes, and then paused to watch a beefy American sailor swing a big wooden mallet in an effort to send a weight shooting up a pole to ring a bell. The figure involved in this attraction was not particularly complimentary to the visitors: the weight traveled straight up the long, lean frame of a sly, foxy-looking Uncle Sam, and if it rang the bell it also tilted Uncle Sam's hat.

"I'll bet your Cousin Ludvig designed that," Nels remarked to Kristine.

After a couple of warm-up tries, the sailor managed the trick. The crowd that had gathered to watch was still applauding when a huge, barrel-chested Swede elbowed his way to the machine like an angry bear and seized the mallet. The crowd moved forward, blocking out the midshipmen's view, but they could hear the blows of the heavy mallet and see the weight slide up. The first two or three times the weight fell short, but then it began to ring the bell regularly.

"Guess he finally hit his stride," observed Oscar. "He was a little weak those first few tries."

Just then Nels caught a glimpse of the big man at work. He uttered a low whistle.

"I hate to tell you, Oscar, but he's swinging that thing with *one hand.*"

Kristine's head went up proudly.

"That's a Swede!"

The one-handed bell-ringer swung twice more for good measure and then tossed down the mallet and pushed out through the crowd, glowering around triumphantly, as though wanting everyone to rejoice over the way he had upheld the honor of Sweden.

"Don't tell me, I can guess. That *is* your cousin," said Nels.

"It is not. My Cousin Ludvig would make two of him."

Close by the Uncle Sam concession was a funhouse known as the *Glaslabyrinten*. It was exactly what its name indicated — a glass labyrinth. Hundreds of mirrors lined a labyrinth that included many dead ends and blind alleys. The mirrors were so arranged that from time to time spectators standing on the outside could see the persons who had gone inside as they struggled to find their way through the maze. They would appear, sometimes apparently close up, sometimes far back, bumping against mirrors, laughing uproariously, and vanishing from sight again as they moved on.

"I could walk through with my eyes shut," said Kristine. "I have been many times, and so has Ulle. Let us see you and Oscar try to go through."

"All right. Shall we show them, Oscar?"

Nels stepped to the ticket window. As he did, Goodman came running up.

"Hey, you guys, I been looking for you!"

"Why?"

"You better get lost, that's why. It's the shore patrol. They're combing the park for midshipmen, with orders to put them under arrest and send them to the Town Hall!"

"You're kidding."

"No, I'm not. I heard them talking. They got troubles

120

down there at the dance. Too many girls, not enough mid-shipmen. Regular international crisis. So the officer in charge at the dance sent out orders to the shore patrol to round up some more midshipmen and send them to the dance pronto."

"You see?" said Kristine. "The girls who went last night also went again tonight."

"But listen, Goodman, we don't have any shore patrol in Goteborg," said Nels. "Mr. Jackson was telling us about it the other day. The Swedish police won't allow us to use our shore patrol in Sweden."

"That's right, so our guys can't wear their armbands — but they're around just the same, on the sly." He pointed. "Lookit, here they come now, and if you don't believe me —"

Nels glanced at the two petty officers Goodman was pointing out. As he did, one of them noticed him and nudged the other.

"Hey! You two middies!"

Nels needed no further convincing. Faced with a crisis, he acted swiftly. He turned and shoved money through the ticket window.

"Two!" he cried. "Come on, Oscar!" And they sprang inside the glass labyrinth like rabbits into a thicket. Goodman melted away into the crowd. The girls stood by the spectators' rail, transfixed, as the two shore patrolmen rushed up.

"Wise guys," snapped the senior man, a first class petty officer. "Go in and get 'em, Armbruster."

"Okay, Suchek."

Armbruster bought a ticket and went inside. In one of the mirrors the spectators outside could see Nels and Oscar appear briefly, bump into a mirror, and then find an opening and disappear again. Suchek gestured at their images menacingly.

"Come outa there, you guys!"

Armbruster appeared, moving like a sleepwalker.

"Armbruster! They went that way!" cried Suchek, pointing left. Armbruster, who obviously could not see him, turned slowly and disappeared to the right. Nels and Oscar reappeared and disappeared again. Armbruster appeared again, still going in the wrong direction. Gales of Swedish laughter rolled from the crowd watching.

"Aw, nuts! I shoulda gone myself in the first place!" muttered Suchek. Giving his sailor pants a hoist fore and aft, and tipping his white hat at an even more self-confident angle, he made for the ticket window.

Kristine stepped forward.

"I know the way through the maze, officer, if you would like help," she said.

Suchek, the man of action, made his move as swiftly as had Nels.

"Two!" he said to the ticket seller, and escorted the helpful Swedish girl inside.

Nels and Oscar made another brief appearance, still wandering. So did Armbruster, though nowhere near them.

Then Kristine appeared, with Suchek behind her.

A moment later Kristine appeared in another place, without Suchek behind her.

Then Suchek appeared elsewhere, alone and red in the face as he pawed about, trying to find an opening.

Next Kristine appeared again, with Nels and Oscar behind her.

Suddenly the three of them came out of the exit and grabbed Ulle's hands on their way past, causing her to fly along with them as they skirted the crowd of onlookers.

"I'd like to stay and see if those guys ever find each other, but I suppose we better not," said Nels.

"Shucks, no. But wait a minute!" Oscar pulled up short in front of Uncle Sam. He slapped down a coin, picked up the mallet, and swung it with one hand, putting every muscle and sinew of his long rawboned frame behind the arc of the thick wooden cylinder.

"*Boing!*" went the bell, and the tall striped silk hat tilted. Nels was astounded. Oscar's gentleness camouflaged extraordinary strength.

"Say! Why didn't you do that before?"

"And spoil that poor Swedish feller's evening? Now, would that have been a nice thing to do?" asked Oscar. "Well, come on — let's skedaddle!"


Outside Liseberg Park they held a hasty council.

"With press gangs out looking for midshipmen, we'd better get off the streets," said Nels.

"My mother and father would be very happy to have us

123

come to my home," said Kristine. "Also, I know my mother did a great amount of baking today."

They had not had anything to eat for more than an hour, so nobody needed any further urging.

The Johnsons lived not far from Gotaplatzen, a handsome square dominated by the Art Gallery and flanked by the City Theater and the Municipal Concert Hall, with an imposing fountain in the center. Rising from the middle of the fountain was a statue of Poseidon, the god of the sea. Oscar's reaction to the nude male figure over which water played unceasingly was typical of one who had spent two weeks at sea on a destroyer, where the amount of fresh water the evaporators can produce is limited and water conservation must be practiced by all hands.

"He's sure going to get in trouble, letting the shower run that long," remarked Oscar.

The Johnsons' apartment was large and comfortable, and Mrs. Johnson's servings of pastry were large and delicious. She knew no English, but her cooking spoke for itself. Mr. Johnson, a civil engineer, spoke English quite well. Although they had a more formal manner than most persons at home in America had under similar circumstances, they made the midshipmen feel welcome. If Kristine's Cousin Ludvig had prejudiced them against America as much as he had Kristine, they did not betray the fact.

To be sure, nobody could have remained stiff and formal for very long with Oscar around. The crooked grin that flashed across his homely face was disarming, and his enthusiasm and friendliness were irresistible because they were genuine. The things he said about Mrs. Johnson's pastry were the same things almost anybody else would have thought of, but the tone of Oscar's voice beat down all language barriers and had her beaming as she filled his plate again.

As for Nels, who tended to be shy and quiet at first, his restraint nicely complemented Oscar's outgoing ways. And after a while it was he who, in telling their adventures in the *Glaslabyrinten,* left the Johnsons wiping their eyes. With Nels telling the story, and Kristine translating for her mother, the room shook with laughter and formality melted away.

Kristine was full of plans.

"Oh, it is very nice that you should be here in Sweden just now, for Midsummer's Eve."

"What's Midsummer's Eve all about, anyway?"

"Don't tell me you don't even know that? On Midsummer's Eve, in the north country, the sun never sets, and even here it will be light all night, of course, the same as tonight."

"When is Midsummer's Eve?"

"Why, day after tomorrow, of course. Except for Christmas, it is our most important festival. Everybody goes out into the country with lots to eat and drink and everybody dances around Maypoles all night long. We will all go to the Gustavsons', and I hope *Fader* will say we may invite you," she said, glancing at her father, "because many of the Americans will be invited. . . ."

125

She paused as she saw the midshipmen exchange a look of concern.

"But perhaps you would not want to come —"

"We'd like very much to come, but we have to go to Copenhagen. We have to leave on the train, day after tomorrow." Nels explained about their tour. "Oscar, I wonder if we could talk some of the other fellows into buying our tickets and going in our place?"

"We could try. I'm willing if you are."

"Oh, but you must see Copenhagen! It is one of the most beautiful cities in the world, even if it is in Denmark," said Kristine, who had quickly adjusted her thinking to this new turn of events. "I love to visit Copenhagen myself. In fact I have an aunt there, my Aunt Berta, who is always asking me to come and spend some days visiting her, and I really should not wait any longer to visit her, and she would be most delighted to have Ulle come with me . . ."

# CHAPTER X

FROM THE OPEN WINDOWS of two railway carriages, one hundred and ten midshipmen watched the green and fertile farmlands of southern Sweden pass by under bright, sunny, midsummer skies.

Gently rolling, with here and there an outcropping of rocky ledges, and dotted with neat frame houses, the land might have been taken for a section of New England.

"Beautiful farmland. Ought to give a good yield." Oscar sighed. "Fair makes a feller homesick for the farm, to see land like that. Except for being rolling instead of flat, and green instead of prairie brown, and cool instead of hot, it reminds me a lot of Kansas."

From flagstaffs in nearly every front yard they passed, the flag of Sweden — a yellow cross on a blue field — marked the national holiday. Once seven flags were in sight at one time. All were the same standard size. In some cases weather had faded the yellow cross to white, but none of the flags were tattered or torn.

"Too bad we had to miss dancing around the Maypole

all night with the girls, ol' buddy. I'm a bug for those native dances."

"I feel guilty about that, Oscar. I'd like to clobber Corny Schultz! If it weren't for him, we'd be on the train coming back today, and we'd get back to Goteborg in time for the fun tonight."

"That's true. But if it wasn't for Corny we wouldn't have met Ulle and Kristine in the first place, and then where would we be?"

"Why, I'm surprised at a playboy like you asking a question like that, Oscar. We'd have met a couple of other girls."

"I suppose so. Still, that Ulle would be hard to beat, even though she wasn't the size I ordered, nor the color of hair. And the way you've been acting I reckon you think Kristine is pretty special, too."

Nels squirmed. "Oscar, I'm ashamed of myself. I admit it. I meant to be true to Eloise in every way, but . . . Well . . . I kissed Kristine on the roller coaster last night. Can you beat it? No will power at all."

Oscar looked complacent. "I'm glad I don't have your problems, ol' buddy. I just leave the will power up to the gals."

A yell went up as a train rushed by going north. Waves were exchanged from the open windows.

"There goes the first tour."

Nels rubbed his hands together. "Just think, Oscar. That's the closest I'm going to be to Schultz this whole week."

At Halsingborg they left the train and boarded a ferry for Helsingor, across the sound in Denmark. On the way over, Herr Wieselgren, the travel bureau official in charge of their party, mentioned Helsingor's greatest claim to fame.

"Helsingor is called Elsinore in English. It is here you will see Kronborg Castle on your sightseeing tour tomorrow. Kronborg Castle, as you know, was the setting for Shakespeare's famous play, *Hamlet*." A slightly superior Swedish smile overcame Herr Wieselgren's face as he added, "The Danes are very obliging about showing the tourist around in the castle. They will even show you Prince Hamlet's grave, and the very pond poor Ophelia drowned herself in — which is remarkable when you consider that both of them were only characters in a play. But then, that's a Dane for you."

In Helsingor Herr Wieselgren pointed out another impressive, though humbler, landmark.

"See that building dated 1641? Ever since it was built it has been a drugstore!"

"Think of that," said Oscar. "Maybe Shakespeare himself dropped in there once for a milkshake and a grilled cheese."

"They don't have soda fountains in drugstores over here," retorted one stuffy midshipman who didn't know a joke when he heard one.

"Well, an aspirin tablet, then," said Oscar. "Maybe rehearsals weren't going so good."

As it grew dark, bonfires appeared on many hillsides.

Herr Wieselgren explained that they were part of the tradition of Midsummer's Eve.

"They are usually laid in the center of a small circle of bushes. This is part of an old custom having to do with burning the witches. If you know someone you don't like, you write his or her name on a piece of paper and throw it into the fire. In this way you destroy your enemy."

Nels pulled out a pencil and nudged Oscar.

"How do you spell Schultz?"

"Forget about Schultz. This is a pleasure trip." Oscar was studying the "Everyday Phrases" given in the *Cruise Ports Guidebook* the midshipmen had received, mumbling them over to himself. "I sure wish I knew some Swedish and Danish. You're lucky, Mr. Wieselgren, being able to speak the language."

Herr Wieselgren's hands went up in protest. "Who can speak the language? I have a terrible time with Danish. Terrible, terrible. It's not the same as Swedish at all, not at all. In fact, whenever I'm in Goteborg and have to telephone a Danish business associate in Copenhagen, it's so bad trying to understand each other over the telephone that we usually give up and speak English. For that matter, although I like Copenhagen, I am not altogether happy when I am there, because you know the Danes don't care very much for the Swedes, and I'm sorry to say it's vice versa with us. Much as I regret to say so, it is vice versa," he repeated, emphasizing this sorrowful statement with a series of sad nods. "They're always complaining about this island and that island we took from them, and things like that — just give any Dane half a chance, and he'll mention them to you —"

"When did you take the islands, Mr. Wieselgren?"

"Oh, a couple of centuries ago. On the other hand, to hear the Danes talk, you'd think we had never suffered from having them meddling in *our* affairs. . . ."

As European cities go, Goteborg was a comparatively new settlement. It had been founded as recently as 1619. Copenhagen was really much older, and now a great metropolis of over a million population. An ancient center of commerce, a great and beautiful capital, it was encrusted with history. Goteborg was a provincial city — clean, attractive, as domestic as a housewife, and not so completely different from home as to look thoroughly foreign to American eyes. In fact, there had been times in certain parts of Goteborg when the boys might have felt as though they were in an American city had not everyone around them been speaking a foreign language.

It was Copenhagen that made Nels and Oscar truly feel the impact of Europe, of an older culture and an older world they had not previously known.

Even if the glories of Copenhagen had not fascinated Nels as they did, Oscar would have enjoyed them enough for two. They left their hotel early in the morning to tramp the streets and snap countless pictures of castles and palaces, of the fish market and the flower market, of swans on the lakes, and of the famous "Little Mermaid" statue on a rock overlooking the harbor. At 10:30, they returned to board a sightseeing bus for a tour of the northern part of Zealand, the island on which the capital city is situated.

Along with their sightseeing at Frederiksborg Castle and Kronborg Castle the midshipmen managed to do plenty of eating. The tour included a stop at a seaside inn for a hearty smorgasbord luncheon which they washed down with Danish beer. Later on, at one of their stops to see an old church, somebody spotted a neighborhood pastry shop. By the time the midshipmen finished buying pastry, the shop was ready to close early. There was not so much as a crumb left to sell.

Everywhere they went as tourists there was one thing the midshipmen were sure to find, and that was other tourists. Copenhagen was jammed with visitors from nearly every country in the world, but above all with Americans. As they returned to the city late that afternoon, several of the midshipmen began discussing the number of their fellow countrymen they had already encountered. The middies were billeted in several hotels, but in each hotel the situation seemed to be the same: all were full of Americans.

"No language problem here," said one midshipman. "Our lobby is loaded with girls all the time, and I haven't met one yet who's Danish. They're all from Chicago."

"Yes, but who wants to pick up American girls when he's in Europe? Not me, brother!"

"Talk about American girls, you should have been with me this morning," said an upperclassman from the *Macon,* named George Bixby. Bixby was billeted in the same hotel as Nels and Oscar. "I came downstairs for breakfast and there, sitting in the lobby and crossing the best pair of legs I'd popped my eyes over yet, was a real doll. Well, I'm half Danish on my mother's side and probably the only guy on this whole tour who can speak the language some, so I thought I'd try it out. *'God Morgen, Froken, hvordan har De det?'* I says to her. That's Danish for 'Good morning, Miss, how are you?' Well, she rolls her eyes up my chest and gives me a come-on look that peels my eyeballs, and what do you think she says to me? 'Greetings, jerk, let's go berserk.' "

Oscar whinnied with amazement. "Well, what do you know? I knew a gal back home who used that expression. She even wrote me a few times after I came to the Academy, but I haven't heard from her for a long time now. Matter of fact, she isn't around home any more. Last time she wrote she said somebody in her family had died and left her some money and she was going to —"

With a gasp Oscar sat up straight in his seat.

"Jumpin' gee-hosaphat! She was going to take a trip to Europe!" He stared at Bixby. "What was this gal's name?"

"I don't know. I was still standing there with my mouth open, and she was laughing at how surprised I looked, when three jet-propelled old ladies came blasting through the lobby and dragged her away with them into a sightseeing limousine."

"What was this girl's voice like?"

"Yours."

Oscar groaned. "What did she look like?"

"S-e-x, boy. Built like a —"

133

"Tall?"

"I was going to mention that. Every bit as tall as I am, she was, and I'm six feet even."

"Dark-haired?"

"Roger."

Oscar had tensed like a stag at the sound of the hunter's horn.

"That's Claribel, sure as shooting."

"Who?"

"Claribel Hatch. We went to high school together."

"Well, I'm a dirty word," said Bixby. "Man, what do you want out of life? If I'd gone to high school with *that* and she turned up within reach *anywhere,* I sure wouldn't be complaining."

"I've got other fish to fry," muttered Oscar. "Besides, Claribel always made me nervous."

Oscar was nervous right now, and the closer they got to the hotel the more nervous he became.

"Listen, Nels, I'm going around and sneak in the back way. You don't know Claribel. Why, if she was to get wind of me being here she'd slap herself onto me like a mustard plaster — and how would it look for us to meet the girls tonight with Claribel Hatch in tow? She's the kind of girl other girls enjoy like a run in their stocking."

Nels had to admit that a fifth wheel was a fifth wheel the world over.

"Okay, Oscar, we'll take the back way, just in case."

They felt a bit foolish slinking around the side of the building to enter by a rear door, but nevertheless Oscar considered the effort well justified when they reached their third-floor corridor without incident.

"You don't know Claribel," he repeated, once they had slipped safely into the entrance hall that served two rooms. As was usually the case in Europe, bathroom facilities were split up. On one side of the entrance hall was a cubicle containing a stall shower. In each private room there was a lavatory, but the shower and toilet were for the use of the occupants of both rooms.

When they entered the hall, they could hear the shower running.

"Feller from the other room must be taking a shower," remarked Oscar. Then he pulled up short in front of their door and snapped his fingers. "Oh, shucks, we plumb forgot about the key."

"I thought you had it."

"No, I gave it in at the desk this morning."

"Well, that's all right, I can go down and get it. After all, Claribel doesn't know me."

Nels hurried downstairs and returned with the key. By then the shower had stopped running.

"Did that fellow come out of the shower yet?" he asked in a low voice as he unlocked their door.

"Not yet."

"Hope he does soon. I'd like to grab a quick one myself."

Nels did not have to wait long. The door opened, and out stepped a tall, dark-haired girl in a white terry-cloth robe. For one split second she stood transfixed, staring with

135

widening eyes at Oscar. Then she let out a yell that should have brought every hog in Denmark to its feet.

"Oscar Tomlinson, you cute ol' thing, you!" she screamed, and pinned him against the wall with her arms tight around his neck.

Oscar was right, thought Nels as he watched. Just like a mustard plaster.

Claribel kissed Oscar with a sound that reminded Nels of a cork coming out of a wine bottle, and briskly took charge.

"Quick, let's get inside before Aunt Bessie comes back," she said, shoving them both into their room ahead of her. She banged the door shut and leaned against it sighing with relief.

"Whew! Honest, she won't hardly let me out of her sight! Oscar, is it ever good to see your funny ol' horse-face again, well I ask you! I've liked to gone crazy on this tour, with nothing but a bunch of old ladies for company. Believe me, you came along just in time!"

Oscar finally found his voice — or at least *a* voice. It certainly wasn't the one Nels was used to hearing from him. The way it squeaked, anybody would have thought he was thirteen years old and still changing over from soprano.

"Well, well. Small world, ain't it, Claribel?"

"It sure is. But here now, we're not minding our manners. Introduce me to your friend, Oscar." Claribel rolled her big dark eyes toward Nels and gave him a once-over

136

that made him feel as if he should have grabbed something to cover himself with. Oscar did the honors, and they shook hands.

From her full lips on down, Claribel was all curves. She had a wide mouth and teeth that were large, white, and perfect. She glowed with good health and animal spirits. She was a real cornfed beauty, the sort who should be chosen Harvest Ball Queen at the state agricultural college — and had been. Even bulky white terry cloth could do nothing to conceal the fact that Claribel possessed a breathtaking figure.

She sat down and crossed her legs, giving him every opportunity to see why they had drawn Midshipman Bixby across the lobby like two electromagnets.

"Well, now, where'll we go? Aunt Bessie always thought a lot of you, Oscar; she'll *have* to let me off the leash for a run long's I'm going to be with you."

Oscar cleared his throat and looked at Nels, but received no aid from that quarter. Nels didn't know what to say, either.

"Well, Claribel — uh —"

Outside, the entrance hall door opened and closed as someone entered.

"Ooh-hoo, Claribel? Have you finished your shower?"

In a flash the girl sprang up and rushed to the rear wall of the room. The shower was on the other side of it. She cupped her hands against the wall and shouted a reply.

"I'll be out as soon as I'm dry, Aunt Bessie!"

"All right, dear." Aunt Bessie continued on into their room. Claribel blew out her breath.

"Thank goodness she's pretty deaf. Well, I've got to go, but now you give me five minutes to dress and then you knock on our door. Say that you happened to find out from the desk clerk we were registered here. Be real nice to Aunt Bessie and sweet-talk her, the way you can, Oscar — and then we'll hightail out of here and take this town like Grant took Richmond. Oh, and if you're worried about money, don't be — that's the one thing I *have* had on this crummy tour. See you later, guys!"

And whereas she had entered the room as noisily as a Chinese New Year celebration, Claribel slipped out of it now as silently as an Indian. Obviously she was a girl who could do anything she put her mind to.

Oscar collapsed onto a bed. He bore small resemblance to the fellow Nels had thought he knew. Oscar Tomlinson was the most resourceful young man Nels had ever met. He had never seemed to be at a loss about anything, until now. But now he looked as though he had met his match, and more.

"I'm licked. I tell you, I'm licked," he declared. "That Claribel. Trouble is, she's crazy about tall men. Big men. Bigger the better. That's why she's always sort of had a crush on me, so to speak."

He jumped up and paced the room.

"Oh, she's really a nice good-hearted gal, even though I *do* think she ought to get married before too much

138

longer. And I do feel sorry for her, having to do all her traveling with a passel of old ladies like her Aunt Bessie. So even though she's a mite nerve wracking to have around for long, I expect I'd do the town with her for a couple of nights if the situation was a little different and I didn't have Oola on my mind. But doggonit, of all places and all times for Claribel Hatch to turn up, this is sure the wrong place and the wrong time!"

Oscar folded up into a chair and appealed to Nels.

"Ol' buddy, *you* tell *me*. We're supposed to meet the gals at the Tivoli about an hour from now. What are we going to do with Claribel?"

Slowly, thoughtfully, Nels shook his head.

"From what I've seen of Claribel," he replied, "I'd say we're going to take her along."

# CHAPTER XI

As THE *Cruise Ports Guidebook* put it, "There is an old saying which goes, 'Denmark means Copenhagen, and Copenhagen means the Tivoli.'"

The Tivoli was one of the finest amusement parks in the world. Unlike most amusement parks, it was in the center of the city's business district, directly across from the railroad station, and a stone's throw from the *Raadhus* Square itself.

More than twenty restaurants, beer halls, and wine shops, along with dance pavilions, bandstands, and concessions of all sorts, filled the space around the borders of a small lake. Fanciful lanterns lighted the walks that circled the lake. Flowers glowed from perfectly kept beds or burst like miniature hanging gardens from large stone bowls suspended beside the walks. Music was always in the air, and festivities concluded at midnight in a lavish fireworks display that set the sky above the park ablaze with light.

Uncertain as to how many extra fireworks displays the Tivoli might be treated to, on this particular evening, Nels and Oscar braced themselves as they approached one of the park's many entrances. Between them, her arms linked through theirs, Claribel Hatch strode along turning the head of every man they passed. As Nels had remarked earlier to Oscar, "Well, you've got to admit she is something to look at."

"She is, at that," Oscar had admitted sadly. "I guess I was just used to her, seeing as I've known her since we were tadpoles."

Claribel all but skipped as they walked alóng. She was like a kid who had been let out of school when she least expected it.

"Oscar, I thought about you the minute I saw all those dreamboats walking around the hotel in these cute uniforms you wear. I even tried to find out if you were on one of the boats here — talked on the telephone to a nice officer who wanted to come right over himself — but I never *dreamed* you'd actually turn up and rescue me like a knight in shining armor." She made a face. "Armor! I've seen so much of that stuff in museums, I wish I hadn't reminded myself of it. I'm getting stoop-shouldered from bending over museum cases. Aunt Bessie never misses a one. And churches! It's got so I look forward to Sunday, because then we generally only go into *one* church instead of three or four like every other day. Honest, Oscar, sometimes I wish we were still poor — and home in Kansas."

"I don't blame you, Claribel. Speaking of money, though, I still don't feel you should —"

"Now, you just forget about that. This is my treat, and

I'm not taking any back talk. I know you boys at the Academy don't have money to burn, so let's not kid around about it." Before they left the hotel Claribel had stuffed a huge handful of Danish *kroner* notes into his pocket as though they were confetti. "I'm glad to do it."

Once inside the Tivoli, they stopped and looked around to get their bearings. Oscar consulted a map he had picked up.

"We're supposed to meet the girls in front of a restaurant called the Wivex. I guess it'll be over thataway."

A subtle little wriggle traveled up Claribel's superb body, as though she were checking all her feminine equipment and finding everything in order. She did not act contemptuous of whatever competition she might be about to meet, nor did she look worried. It was Oscar who was looking worried. As she glanced into a compact mirror and powdered her nose, he eyed her nervously.

"Now, Claribel, remember what you promised. When I introduce Oola, don't you hang on my arm and go crawling up it like you own me, or anything like that."

"Oscar, don't you worry," said Claribel looking almost demure. "I'm sure I'm going to like Oola a lot."

They found the Wivex, but the girls were nowhere in sight. Oscar breathed an audible sigh of relief.

"It's just putting things off, but still I'm glad we're here first and I can sort of get set. Doggonit, Claribel, you're a gal, you can understand how they'll feel. It's asking a lot of a couple of females to have them come all the way down from Goteborg to Copenhagen to be with us, and then have us turn up with another female."

"Listen, I came about five thousand miles to be here myself, didn't I?"

"Not specially to be with me, you didn't, Claribel —"

"Oh-oh," said Nels. "Here they come."

The girls' faces were something to see as they spied their two midshipmen. To begin with, they had been hurrying along glancing back over their shoulders as though the police were after them. Then, when they saw the boys, their pretty faces lit up with broad smiles that froze and dwindled away as they took note of the girl between them. For of course the minute Nels said, "Here they come," Claribel linked arms again with both boys.

"Kristine!" cried Nels.

"Oola!" quavered Oscar.

They all but pulled Claribel off her feet as with one accord they stepped forward to welcome the girls, who scarcely gave them a glance, so busy were they in sizing up Claribel. Oscar quickly stumbled through the introductions and began to explain.

"Claribel's from back home, and she just happened to be in town on this here European tour she's taking, so we said we were sure you wouldn't mind if —"

By then the bewildered girls had recovered themselves enough to remember that they had problems of their own. Kristine tugged at Nels's coat sleeve.

"Come, we must go away from here as fast as we can! We must talk somewhere else."

"What's the matter?"

Her blue eyes were round with fright.

"Guess who *we* found at my Aunt Berta's?"

"Who?"

"Cousin Ludvig!"

"What?"

"Yes! His ship is here now. And he knows we came here to meet you, and he is furious, like a wild man, because you know how he feels about Americans. He said he will follow us, and if he finds us with any American midshipmen he will knock their heads together! Please, we must hurry, because I am sure he followed us, and if he finds us it will be terrible. He has such a temper, that one; and he's so big and strong — like nobody you ever saw!"

"He *is?*" asked Claribel.

Her tone caused Nels and Oscar to exchange a glance of wild surmise. They had started to walk along with the girls, but now Oscar stopped short.

"Wait. What makes you so sure Cousin Ludvig followed you?"

"I am certain I saw him. Two or three times, on the way here."

"Well, now, let's take another look." Oscar peered at the crowd in the direction from which the girls had come.

"Oscar, *please!*"

"Wow! Look at the size of *that* feller!" he remarked. "Is that him?"

Plowing through the crowd came what looked like one of the original Norse gods in person. All he needed was a

144

bearskin and a battle-ax. The frown on his huge face scattered ordinary human beings out of his path like sparrows.

"That's him!"

"By golly, you weren't kidding about the size of him, were you, Kristine? Claribel, did you ever see a more impressive hunk of manhood than that in all your born days?"

Claribel couldn't even speak. She was too busy breathing deeply.

"Nels, you take a feller with Cousin Ludvig's anti-American leanings — what he needs is to be exposed to a real stemwinder of an American girl for a while," mused Oscar. "That'd take some of the wind out of his sails."

It was the old Oscar who stepped forward now. A man who was sure of himself, and never at a loss.

A hearty smile of welcome wreathing his homely face, Oscar surprised the Norse god with a cheery beckoning wave.

"Hey, Cousin Ludvig! Come here!" he cried. "We've got somebody we want you to meet!"

Their visit to Copenhagen had been gay from beginning to end, but in a matter of minutes, now, the great city would be just a happy memory.

The midshipmen had finished an enormous lunch, with smorgasbord followed by a main course, at one of the hotels. Herr Wieselgren and Lieutenant Rowen, the officer in charge of the party, were both rushing around anxiously, trying to make sure nobody was missing. Outside, the buses were waiting to take them to the railroad station.

Before rising from the table, Nels and Oscar raised their beer glasses and clicked them together for a few final toasts.

"Well, here's to Copenhagen, long may she wave," said Oscar.

"And here's to Ulle and Kristine, may we never forget them," said Nels.

"And here's to Claribel, for that matter," added Oscar. "She sure took care of Cousin Ludvig. That big Swede will never be the same."

"Good old Lamby," said Nels, that being the pet nickname Claribel had ultimately saddled him with. They drained their glasses and sadly set them down. Oscar sighed.

"I sure am going to miss this town, and those girls. I want to tell you, that Oola would be hard to beat. Her folks are fine, too. My kind of farm people, they are. Yes, sir, ol' buddy, I don't mind saying, I feel pretty miserable right now. I figured my motto was love 'em and leave 'em, but — well, the lovin' is easier than the leavin'."

A few minutes later the contingent of midshipmen boarded the train. Herr Wieselgren and Mr. Rowen bustled through the cars taking a head count and then collapsed into a seat and congratulated each other on the total: one hundred and ten.

Oscar took off his cap and tossed it on the rack above their seat. Nels started to do the same with his, but paused to gaze inside it. Inside his dress cap was a favorite place for a midshipman to carry a picture of his best girl.

146

Nels held the cap before them while he and Oscar contemplated the picture silently. Then Oscar nodded.

"No getting around it, that Kristine is a mighty pretty girl."

Once again, Nels squirmed guiltily.

"I shouldn't have treated Eloise this way, but what could I do? Kristine spotted Eloise's picture, and asked me about it, and then asked me if I'd like to have *her* picture to keep in my cap. What could I say? Anyway, I'll be honest with you, I did want it." One last look, and then he dutifully changed the pictures around, slipping Kristine's under Eloise's. Eloise seemed to eye him accusingly.

"Well, I'll try to do better in Hamburg," he promised aloud.

"I don't see how you could do better than Kristine."

"All right, wise guy, that's not what I meant!"

On the best of tours there are always a few minor mix-ups. In this case, the box lunches for the return journey, which were supposed to come aboard the train in Sweden, came aboard in Copenhagen instead.

These box lunches were not skimpy affairs. They contained four good sandwiches, complete with mayonnaise and butter; two tomatoes; several radishes, and some lettuce; two hard-boiled eggs, halved; salt; and a piece of Danish pastry. Besides this, each man received a bottle of orange drink, and a plastic bag containing an orange and a banana.

The midshipmen had scarcely settled themselves in their

147

seats before the box lunches were passed out. Nels and Oscar examined theirs absent-mindedly and reacted automatically to the sight of food. They began to eat. With methodical thoroughness they demolished one sandwich after another, one egg after another, one tomato after another. All around them, other middies were doing the same.

Herr Wieselgren, a middle-aged man who had a nervous stomach and a limited appetite, watched them with incredulous eyes and turned a bit green at their praying mantis appetites.

"But we only just finished lunch!" he groaned. "How can you do it?"

Oscar glanced at him with surprise.

"Why, shucks, Mr. Wieselgren," he said between bites, "there isn't hardly ever a time when I can't nibble at a snack like this."

Three more letters from Eloise were waiting for Nels when they reached the *Morton*. They were full of tender phrases that made him feel guiltier than ever about all the happy hours he had spent in Kristine's company. True, they contained several more references to that fellow Ronald — he always seemed to be around when there was tennis, sailing, or picnics going on — but considering the way Nels had been passing the time himself, he felt he should overlook Ronald. After all, Eloise was telling him all about it and not concealing anything, which was more than he could say for himself. His letters from Copenhagen had been particularly skimpy, and somehow he had not brought himself to dwell on the fact that there was a special Swedish girl in the picture.

"I'd feel a lot worse," he confided to Oscar, "if I didn't have those cashmere sweaters to take home to her."

Oscar's long face assumed that solemn-old-horse look again. "And you call *me* a playboy!" he said.

# CHAPTER XII

ALL DURING THAT ENDLESS MIDWATCH the North Sea squirmed and tossed like a restless sleeper with a short temper. The *Morton's* situation was made more difficult by the fact that she and the other ships from Goteborg were ahead of schedule. Consequently they were poking along at seven knots, wallowing in the crochety seas instead of driving through them, as they approached a rendezvous with the ships from Oslo.

Despite having passed into his Engineering phase, Nels was standing the watch on the bridge. Because of an earlier switch in watches, he was thus privileged to participate in what was one of the worst midwatches of the cruise.

Winter or summer, the temperature of the North Sea varied little. It was always cold. After the week of summer weather they had enjoyed ashore, the damp chill of the sea prickled its way into the marrow of every man's bones, even through the heavy foul-weather jackets.

The forward deck was constantly awash. Now and then the bow plunged and sent a wall of gray-green water up to smash against the windows of the bridge. Spindrift sheered off to port in great sheets, torn to tatters by a howling wind.

Standing by in a corner of the pilothouse, wearing the headphones of the JA circuit during the wet, cold, uneventful hours, was the kind of duty that seemed to stretch seconds into minutes and minutes into hours. Nels would have welcomed another trick at the wheel. There, at least, one had a fight on one's hands. Constant spinning of the wheel was necessary to hold the ship anywhere nearly on course in such a sea. It was more a matter of bracketing the course, checking the ship's swings, keeping those swings within as narrow a range as possible.

No, having the wheel was not so bad. It was this standing around with nothing to do, and with nothing happening, that was hard to endure. One's feet ached, vitality ebbed, and the cold penetrated that much more. Time needed killing, and weapons were few. The ship seemed to be going nowhere, and doing it in the most uncomfortable way. Their position changed with agonizing slowness. When he had first come on watch, a distant bright beacon — ashore on Jutland — had been on their port bow. All through the watch it had been there, turning, turning, and even now it was scarcely more than abeam.

Nels did his best to pass the time by thinking about home, about Eloise, about his father, and about the fact that only a little more than a month remained now of the cruise, and of his days in the Navy.

After a foot-loose week of liberty ashore, it had been like returning to prison to come back to the narrow confines and regimentation of the ship. He had dreaded the return to routine, the reports to Corny Schultz, and the possibility of a fresh bout with seasickness. Then, too, there were those two appearances at mast, which should be coming before long now, to worry about. How would he make out on those? How would they look on his record? What would his father think?

That was what mattered, of course — his father. It was because of him that Nels wanted to make at least a creditable showing on this cruise. He wanted to resign from the Academy with honor, and not with any appearance of being on the verge of failure anyway. Since the spud locker episode and Mr. Jackson's warning words, Nels had worked hard, harder than he had ever dreamed he might. In this effort he had been helped by Oscar and even by the sharp and unremitting surveillance provided by Corny Schultz. Corny had meant it when he assured Nels he intended to make certain he produced. He seemed determined, through Nels, to show Mr. Jackson a thing or two himself.

Returning to the ship, then, had depressed Nels greatly. But oddly enough, the depression had not been justified by events. He found himself taking the now familiar routine in stride, and feeling thereby like something of an old sea dog. This feeling increased almost to one of cheerfulness when he found his stomach stoutly resisting the surly attempts of the North Sea to upset it. A sort of springy-footed exhilaration surprised him as he strode about the small ship that was so much a part of the sea, and for the first time he was attacked by that sense of cocky superiority that is part of a tin-can sailor when he looks across tossing waves from his bouncing cork of a ship and spies one of those stodgy floating hotels, the cruisers and battleships. Why, those guys over there didn't know what it was to be at sea!

Even Corny Schultz had not managed to be as insufferable as usual.

"Well, Crane, I must say my arrangements worked out delightfully. I certainly enjoyed spending seven glorious days without you in the picture."

"Yes, sir."

"And vice versa, no doubt."

"Whatever you say, sir."

"How kind of you to spare my feelings. Tell me, are you planning to take the tour up the Rhine to Frankfort when we get to Hamburg?"

"No, sir."

"Too bad. Neither am I. I really think you should go."

"I can't afford it, sir."

"Neither can I." Corny sighed. "Well, it's a big city. Now then, Crane, I want to see your assignment on Radiological Defense finished and ready to hand in by this evening. . . ."

One reason none of the things he had dreaded seemed as bad as he had expected, Nels decided, was the knowledge that there was only one week of shipboard routine to be gotten through before they would reach Hamburg and another full week of relative freedom. As was usual in port, liberty would not begin until 1300 each day, and would end for third classmen at 0100. Workday routine would

153

prevail during the morning hours. It would not be like Copenhagen, but it would be good enough.

A flurry of activity on the bridge broke the chain of Nels's thoughts. From the *Macon* came the order for a change of course. It was passed on by the OOD to the helmsman.

"Come right to two six five."

"Right to two six five. Aye aye, sir."

Through the speaking tube connected to the captain's sea cabin abaft the pilothouse the officer of the desk reported the change of course.

"Captain . . ." And when the captain, roused from his customary light sleep, had quickly answered, the OOD said, "We have a change of course, sir. Right to two six five."

Nels visualized the tiny sea cabin, but instead of Captain Penn he saw his father there. How many times during his long years at sea had his father been awakened like that? How often had he been forced to snatch sleep forty winks at a time, and how often during the war years had he gone for days on end with no sleep at all? Why did a man knowingly let himself in for such a wretched existence, living for weeks at a time in a cramped cube of space that fifty-foot dimensions would have enclosed? Only in port did he get away from his ship, and even then it was always on his mind. At sea, except for an hour or so during Saturday inspections of the ship and personnel, the captain seldom strayed fifty feet from the bridge. The wardroom for meals and the evening movie, the sea cabin for sleep, and the bridge the rest of the time; this was his world at sea. This had been his father's world, and this would some-day be Perry's, when Perry reached the lonely distinction of command. But not his. He admired them, and he admired Captain Penn, but they were crazy, all of them. Crazy to put up with it.

There had been another letter from his father waiting for him when he returned to the ship. All three of his father's letters had touched him deeply because of the things they left unsaid, things that stuck out plainly between every line: the hope that he was being won over, the hope that some miracle would make him change his mind about the Navy. At times Nels almost wished he could, but then his old bitterness would come flooding back and leave an acrid taste in his mouth as he thought of all that had happened to his father — and to his mother.

First, there had been the lonely peacetime months and wartime years when his father had been away at sea. Then, when one of the consolations of forced retirement had been that at least now they could be together all the time, she had been taken from him, taken from them all, by a cruel and senseless illness, a swift blow that had all but destroyed Nels's faith in anything.

Rather than brood on the past — for he had been learn-ing, slowly and painfully, how dangerous and profitless this can be — Nels forced his thoughts to turn to the fu-ture, to Eloise, and to what fun it would be to live in New York someday and be like his Uncle Matt, with a terrific apartment in midtown Manhattan, a big job, and all sorts of celebrities for his friends. He did not get far with this pleasant picture, though, because his guilt over not having been altogether true to Eloise began to occupy his mind.

How should he handle the question of how much to tell her about his gay week in Sweden and Denmark? His letters to her so far had been fairly full of museums, castles, and other educational and cultural highlights of his visits ashore. But certainly a letter was no place to go into a delicate subject such as his friendship with another girl, and a Swedish blonde at that. Later on, when he and Eloise were together again and the cruise was all past history, he could tell her all about everything that had happened. She might get a bit mad at first about some of it, but she would have to laugh at it all in the end.

Nels chuckled to himself as he thought back over some of the happenings, such as their adventures in Copenhagen, and Oscar's superb handling of the Claribel Hatch and Cousin Ludvig situations. *By George, I wouldn't have missed it, Eloise or no Eloise!* he found himself thinking, and was a trifle ashamed of this unrepentant surge of high spirits. *I've been around the old cornball too much,* he told himself with an inward grin. *That love 'em and leave 'em attitude of his — it's beginning to rub off on me.* Well, things would be different when he and Eloise could be together again, and in the meantime perhaps it wouldn't hurt him, as Oscar insisted, to see a little something of other places and other girls. He had always been rather shy around girls, and certainly knowing Kristine had helped him feel more confidence in himself.

"Hey, you know something, Crane? This is the strongest wind we've had so far on the cruise."

One of the other third classmen, speaking to him in a low voice, broke into his thoughts. Nels removed one earpiece, sliding it ahead of his ear, so that he could hear better, and said, "It's pretty stiff, all right."

"I just figured out our true wind speed on the maneuvering board. What's your guess?"

"Gee, I don't know. Twenty-five?"

"Twenty-eight. Our relative wind speed's forty; true wind speed, twenty-eight knots." On the maneuvering board, given the ship's speed and course and the wind's direction, the problem was easily solved with compass and parallel rules.

The sky was brightening steadily now. It had never grown really dark at all. By 0130 the sky had begun to lighten in the east, and before 0330 standard time the sun would be rising. Only a few stars had shone at all, for a brief time around midnight — the great triangle of Vega, Altair, and Deneb, and one or two others. The planet Jupiter had been a brightly glowing orb near a gibbous moon that was still shining brightly, as it had all night long. In the distance, across the sea, the riding lights of a skunk or two appeared, twinkled out, and reappeared as the ships rode up and down the waves and troughs of the sea. Onshore, the beacon continued to turn, flashing and dimming in its steady sweep.

157

Somebody nudged him — "How about some java?" — and handed him a steaming mug of coffee. "Man, if this is summertime in the North Sea I don't want to see it in the winter."

"Only in a good movie," grinned Nels. "Thanks, pal."

The hot brew warmed him to his toes, and the comradeship warmed him, too. It was after three o'clock now, the back of the watch was broken, and suddenly he felt curiously contented, almost lighthearted, almost happy without cause. The sea in that strange morning light was tough, beautiful, and fascinating, and he was a man who had stood a hard watch with the rest of them. It was a small, everyday accomplishment, but still it was something to be able to say you had undergone the experience. Even after he was out of the Navy and all this was past he knew he would be proud of a few small, everyday things such as this.

Oscar had, of course, been gathering information on Hamburg. From the *Cruise Ports* book, from a magazine article he had got wind of and run down, and from members of the crew who had been there before, he had managed to put together a pretty fair idea of their next port.

"Well, I don't know what we're liable to run into there, ol' buddy," he declared, "but I reckon you may have to give me another one of your famous lessons in how to resist females, because they say the place is full of 'em. One nice thing, it'll give me a chance to try out my German. That's my language at the Academy, you know."

158

Each midshipman had to choose a foreign language as one of his courses.

"Mine's French, but I won't get to Paris to try it out," said Nels. "Ninety-nine dollars for four days there, plus whatever extra you'd spend on your own — that's too rich for my blood."

"Mine, too. Too rich for everybody's, I guess, for that matter. I understand that tour's been canceled. Nobody wants to spend that much. Also the tour to Kiel — that's out, too. I guess that one's too much of a busman's holiday — shipyards and the canal, and all that. Only tour that's still going is the one up the Rhine. I wouldn't have minded that, but even with the monthly insult I'd still be cutting things mighty close to spend that extra money."

"The monthly insult" was the name the midshipmen gave to their payday.

"Don't worry, we'll find plenty to do in Hamburg, Oscar."

The lanky farm boy cocked his head to shoot a knowing glance at Nels.

"From what I read about this night club street they have there — the Reeperbahn, it's called — my only worry is that you might find *too* much to do there. Have you ever sat around drinking beer while five or six gals were up on a stage taking off their clothes?"

Nels pretended to yawn nonchalantly.

"Well, naturally. Dozens of times, old boy."

"Haw! You haven't ever done any such a thing, not once," said Oscar. "But brace yourself, boy — because you're going to now!"

159

If the Navy had wanted to choose its cruise ports for purposes of contrast, it could not have done better than to select Goteborg and Hamburg.

Seventy-five miles up the Elbe River, Hamburg was a world shipping center, a great, teeming, cosmopolitan port with the waterfront dives, dirt, and smells of the kind of port the sailors were used to. Its harbor was packed with ships from all the seven seas, with the flags of twenty nations flying from their sterns. British, French, Danish, Swedish, Norwegian, Brazilian, Panamanian, Greek, and Icelandic ships were there. From the staff of one big freighter floated the Star and Crescent of Turkey. The bow of another carried her name in Arabic, repeated below in English; and on the stern of a third the name appeared in Japanese characters, also repeated below in English.

The trip up the Elbe, beginning in a thick pea-souper of a fog and ending in gray mid-morning light, was cause for another voluntary all-night vigil on the part of Nels and Oscar. There is no lack of interest and even tension on the bridge whenever a ship is negotiating a river channel at night and in a fog. Freighters held in port all afternoon and evening were beginning to pick their way down the river, slipping past like black wraiths, and for a while the situation was, as Navy slang expressed it, a hairy one.

Then, as the fog began to lift and the light strengthened, they were able to catch their first glimpses of Germany. Even though they had been mere tots at the time of World War II, it still gave them a strange feeling to look at the land about them and remember that this was enemy territory such a few short years in the past, and that not so long ago their trip up the river would have been suicidal.

The northern bank of the Elbe was lined with steep hills covered with inns and private villas. The flat southern bank of the river was less prepossessing. Here, where there was anything, there were factories and military installations, and here the scars of war still gashed the landscape. Like ugly warts the cracked and battered pillboxes and bunkers marked the places where gun crews had watched and waited. The shells of bombed-out factory buildings — crumbling walls of scarred, fire-blackened red brick, with smashed windows and no roofs — stood in weed-grown desolation. At one point an immense concrete slab, acres of it, battered but still in place, covered what had once been the submarine pens in which U-boats had found shelter.

Alongside the river rose the city of Hamburg, with the damaged spires of its churches providing a further reminder that this was a city in which three hundred thousand buildings had been wrecked by bombings and a hundred and fifty thousand persons had been killed. Hamburg had made mighty strides toward rebuilding, but in some sections the great gaps between houses still stood out like missing teeth.

When Nels and Oscar set foot ashore in a dismal rain, their first impressions of the city were equally dismal. Like Goteborg, Hamburg was a city of canals, but its canals were dirty and smelled bad. In many places the usual drabness of streets near a waterfront was intensified by the ugliness of fire-blackened walls. One warehouse eight

161

stories high had had its back wall partly sheared off, and the sagging building had never been pulled down, but was still partially in use. In level places high up on the broken walls, tangles of green weeds grew. On the fifth floor, cardboard cartons of goods were piled high, under cover of a roof but with no rear wall to protect them.

"Guess they don't figure on rain driving in from that direction," commented Oscar. "But they sure must get it from every other. I heard that second river pilot that came aboard say it had rained here nearly every day for six months! Look at the way those people are walking along. You can tell they've got used to walking in the rain."

The appearance of the people provided another unhappy contrast. Where good looks had been a commonplace in Goteborg, they were a rarity in Hamburg. When they were not talking or smiling, the people here too often wore a severe expression that made them sour and unattractive.

"They're not unfriendly, though," Oscar pointed out. "They just look that way *all* the time."

Certainly the people of Hamburg did not stand aloof or spare the welcome to these foes of a mere dozen years ago. As had been done in Sweden, visitors were allowed aboard the ships and, like the Swedes, the Germans flocked to the landing pier, lining up and waiting patiently to come aboard. Both of the cruisers and a division of destroyers had come to Hamburg. The *Des Moines,* tied up alongside a pier, received the bulk of the visitors. The destroyers and the *Macon* were moored to dolphins out in the harbor, and only a few boatloads of visitors were brought out to visit them. But all day long, every day of their stay in port, scores of sightseeing boats puttered slowly past the warships, and smiling Germans waved vigorously, until waving back to them became a positive chore for the men on deck.

*"Now station waving detail, now station waving detail,"* became a standard joke at Hamburg.

The ships arrived on July 3.

"Seems like a funny place to spend the Fourth of July," Nels declared. "I guess you noticed, by the way, that we're on the list assigned to that party at the American Consulate tomorrow afternoon." There were several official functions and receptions on the program, and the midshipmen had been parceled out amongst the lot of them. "What kind of party is it going to be, anyway?"

"A cocktail party."

"Say!"

"You will be expected to conduct yourself as an officer and a gentleman —"

"How can I be two different things at once?"

"Please, no old jokes, bud. As an officer and a gentleman, I said. You all are in a foreign country now, repussentin' the Yew-nited States Govviment," added Oscar, doing his best imitation of Mr. Jackson, "and I expect you all to act accordin'ly. I will not tolerate et cetera, et cetera . . ."

At Hamburg three letters from Eloise were waiting for Nels. Only three, but on the other hand this time they made no mention of Ronald at all, which pleased Nels.

"Probably he tried to get too serious," he suggested.

"At any rate, she had Ronald, and I had Kristine, and now that's all behind us, so that's fair enough."

He felt a lot better about life, and wrote Eloise a long letter the first chance that came his way.


In the square before the *Rathaus,* the two military bands faced each other, one German, the other American. To the tune of a Sousa march played by the American band, five hundred midshipmen marched stolidly through the rain and formed rank upon rank in the center of the square. Around the sides of the square, German civilians packed the pavement and stood on tiptoe to peer over the front rows of onlookers.

When the midshipmen had formed, the German bandmaster saluted, turned, and brought down his baton. Across the square from the horns and trumpets and drums of the German band swelled the measures of "The Star-spangled Banner." The anthem rolled to its climax, ended, and was applauded by the onlookers.

The American bandmaster saluted, turned, and brought down his baton. From the horns and trumpets and drums of the American band came the sweet, sentimental, Teutonic notes of a German anthem, while, all over the square, felt hats were snatched off and clapped to German breasts.

Then, to a quick march played by the German band, the midshipmen marched into the *Rathaus* for an official welcome from the city of Hamburg.

# CHAPTER XIII

THE REEPERBAHN was the main street of Hamburg's entertainment district. Like Broadway in New York City, however, its name had come to mean more than a street. When anybody spoke of the Reeperbahn, he generally had in mind the entire district of night clubs, cabarets, beerhalls and brothels.

Nels and Oscar began their investigations of the Reeperbahn in the respectable confines of a large beerhall, where family parties were numerous and where beer drinking and band music provided the entertainment.

When they arrived, every seat on the main floor was taken. The two midshipmen found a table by the rail of the balcony that circled the hall. Below them the crowd, mostly German civilians with a sprinkling of the visiting Americans, were seated at long wooden tables. The band musicians, dressed in Bavarian leather shorts, occupied a stage at the head of the hall. In front of the stage a sizable dance floor was filled with couples jammed together and bobbing up and down to the "Oompah" strains of the fifteen-piece band.

"Everything is march music. They even *dance* to it here," Nels observed.

Buxom waitresses wove their way expertly between the tables carrying six huge steins of beer in each hand. Laughing and singing, the citizens of Hamburg had left their severe expressions at home, and looked the better for it. Everybody sang, and did so without the self-consciousness that usually afflicts Americans when they attempt a community sing. At one point the band played a song that involved everyone's standing first on his chair and finally on the tables. Young and old, from students to grandmothers, every last person made the climb and stood on the tables with arms linked, swaying to the music as they roared out the song.

From time to time the musicians filed down from the bandstand and paraded around the hall, led by the bandmaster holding his baton high, looking about for someone to present it to. When some happy reveler had been found who was willing to accept the baton and have the bandmaster's Bavarian hat with a huge feather sticking out of its band put on his head, the honorary bandmaster was led to the stage to conduct a couple of numbers.

In return for the honor that had been bestowed on him, each amateur bandmaster was required to buy a round of beers for the musicians so that his splendid performance could be properly toasted.

"Well, this is a fine place," said Oscar. "Some night I wouldn't mind spending a whole evening here."

"Neither would I."

166

"But not tonight. Tonight we've got a lot of places to see before 0100. You take that place I read about in that magazine piece. That three-in-one place. I'm curious to see that one. I think we ought to get there tonight."

"Some of the fellows say it's quite worth while in a raunchy sort of way."

"Well, ol' buddy, what are we here in Europe for if not to get educated? Let's go!" They rose and clicked their steins together. *"Prosit!"*

One of the Reeperbahn's stellar attractions was a mammoth establishment with three night clubs under one roof. Two of them were in identical large halls that adjoined one another. The third was downstairs.

"Let's try this one first," suggested Oscar, leading the way into one of the halls. "I think this is the one where the gals wrestle in the mud."

"Do what?"

"Also the one with the phones."

"Mud? Phones? What's all this?"

"You'll see, ol' buddy."

The big dimly lit room was long and narrow, with a balcony divided into discreetly private alcoves running around three sides of it. The main floor was filled with tables and booths, and at the end of the room there was a curtained stage.

The boys chose a table, ordered beer, and studied their surroundings. This was a night club with numerous special features. Each table had a small lamppost attached to it, and on the glass panes of the square lamps a number was displayed. A telephone stood on each table. In order to call another table one had only to dial its number.

"This sure gets the pick-up down to a science. If you're feeling sociable and notice a couple of cuties sitting alone at another table, all you have to do is give 'em a ring and see if they'd like to drop over for a visit," said Oscar, looking around.

"Quite a system," nodded Nels, looking around.

"Isn't it?" agreed Oscar, still looking around.

"See anything?"

"Nope. Do you?"

"No. Wait, I take that back."

"Oh, boy."

"See 'em?"

"Yep."

"Not bad."

"Nope."

"Floozies, of course," said Nels in his most worldly manner.

"Well, they don't look like they sing in the village choir, if that's what you mean."

In a state of suppressed excitement, they consulted across the table.

"Shall we give 'em a ring, Nels? I mean, just for fun?"

"Well, sure — but what if they come over? Gee, I wish I knew some German like you do. About all I know is *Ja* and *Nein*."

"Just stick to *Nein* and you'll be safe, ol' buddy. Besides, they probably know English."

"Maybe. But you heard about Nolan's complaint back in Goteborg, didn't you? He said he met a beautiful Swedish girl who only knew one word of English, and that was 'No.'"

"Yes, but I'll bet these two gals never heard of the word. Hey, they're looking this way now."

"I think they're talking about us, Oscar."

"They sure act like it. Say! They're not even waiting for a phone call! Here they come!"

Nels and Oscar exchanged a flustered glance and then sat back in their chairs, each trying to arrange himself in a suitable man-of-the-world pose. Nels's throat had gone dry. His heart was thumping. He wondered if Oscar felt as nervous as he did.

The girls undulated up in their tight skirts and tight blouses and stopped beside the table. With a crooked smile on her painted lips and a twinkle in her mascaraed eyes, one of them reached down and took Nels's chin in her hand. An electric tingle pulsed down his spinal cord and zigzagged out through his toes.

"Hello, baby," she said in a throaty voice. "Does your mother know you're out?"

With that the girls threw their heads back and laughed noisily as they went on to join a couple of flashy-looking middle-aged men who were obviously expecting them a few tables further on. Nels's face glowed like a hot plate.

"The nerve of that dame! Ha ha ha, very funny," he snapped, breaking into a grudging grin as Oscar went into a knee-slapping fit of laughter.

"Doggonit, I shouldn't be traipsing around with anyone that looks so fresh out of the egg," said Oscar, wiping his eyes. "Spoils my chances."

"Fine thing! That silly *Fräulein* must get her slang out of old American magazines. 'Does your mother know you're out?'! Why, that crack was old stuff in the First World War." And Nels made a mental note to start raising a mustache as soon as he was out of the Academy.

"Well, simmer down, child, because it looks like the show's about to start," said Oscar. A fanfare had sounded, and now a girl had thrust her head out of the curtain and was making an announcement.

"What's she saying, Oscar?"

"She says the wrestlers are going to entertain us. Wow! I guess she means it."

The girl wrestlers had appeared. Both were wearing just two items of clothing. One item was a bathing cap.

In front of the stage, the space customarily occupied by an orchestra pit had been converted into another kind of pit — a pit full of mud.

The girls climbed into the pit and went to work. They made a great show of snarling at one another and making loud personal remarks and acting very angry. As Oscar pointed out, though, that magazine article had emphasized that the girls did not really care which of them was declared the winner, and were actually good friends and often sat around knitting shawls and other homey articles for each other between performances.

"Well, I've got to hand it to the Navy," said Oscar. "I never thought I'd see anything like this in my whole life, yet here I am, sitting in Hamburg, Germany, watching two gals with practically no clothes on throw each other over their shoulders and slap each other down into a bunch of mud! You take back in Kansas, now — our gals never seem to go in much for this kind of thing, so I never had an opportunity like this before."

After a while the girls got down out of sight behind the wall of the pit and went into what was supposed to be the really hilarious part of the act. This consisted of flinging handfuls of mud into the air out toward the audience.

"I'm not sure I dig the German sense of humor," said Nels, watching globs of mud fly past.

"Never mind. Just keep ducking."

The show concluded to a spattering of applause and the two midshipmen moved on to another club, the one downstairs. They walked down a flight of steps into an atmosphere that grew increasingly musty.

"Smells like a menagerie."

"Takes me back to the farm," said Oscar.

In its way this second night club was even more bizarre than the first. The center of the room was given over to a small riding ring, and in the ring were some horses, two donkeys, and a camel. The customers sat drinking beer at tables around the sides. When and if the urge seized them, they were permitted to ride any of the animals in the ring.

"Well, it's interesting, but I'm in no mood to ride a camel around in a circle right now," said Oscar. "What say we try the third one? We might as well see it all."

The third night club was an anticlimax. First they saw movies of girls doing artistic dances with almost no clothes on. Then two live girls came on stage and did some in-artistic dances with almost no clothes on, and they proved to be the same girls the boys had seen in the first night club. Oscar yawned.

"Shucks, who wants to watch the same naked gals all over again? What say we shove off?"

A couple of night clubs and fifteen nude girls later, they were standing in a side street reading an advertising folder a man had handed them and trying to decide whether to take in one more place or not. The advertisement was for "International Cabaret Indra"; it offered "fishing for the underwear from the alluring body of young Venus."

"We've seen 'em take their clothes off every other way, maybe we ought to try fishing 'em off," said Oscar. "Some-how, though, it's all beginning to seem like more of the same."

But Nels was not listening. He had noticed a midship-man walking down the other side of the street. The mid-shipman had red hair, and the blonde on his arm was by all odds the prettiest girl Nels had seen in Hamburg.

"Well, it had to happen sooner or later. Look who's there, Oscar. First time I've run into him ashore, and now when I do it's enough to spoil my evening. Where did a guy like him find a dish like that?"

"I don't know, but I sure wish there was a second helping for me."

"Why do jerks like that always get all the breaks?"

"I don't know. All I know is, they're heading away from the night club district, which is funny."

"What do you mean, funny? She's probably invited him to come home with her. If they turn in somewhere together, I'm going to cut my throat. I can't stand to think of Corny Schultz making out that well."

"I hope he isn't going to do anything foolish," said Oscar seriously. "I sure wouldn't want to mess around with any of these Reeperbahn cuties, good-looking or not."

"Well, the guy's twenty-one years old. It's his life."

"That's right. Come on, though, I want to keep an eye on him for a minute," said Oscar, gazing thoughtfully up the street. Nels fell into step beside him, but not without protest.

"Now, wait, Oscar, we can't go tagging along spying on him like a couple of kids."

"I don't mean to. It's those two fellers walking along behind them there that I'm interested in," Oscar explained. He indicated a burly pair fifty feet behind Corny and his girl friend. "Seems to me they're sort of following Schultz. So maybe we better sort of follow them."

Nels grinned, but not very hopefully. "That would be too good to be true. If I thought that girl was playing Schultz for a sucker and setting him up to be rolled, I'd feel better about life. But I'll bet you those two guys will just keep on going. They're probably on the night shift in a brewery somewhere."

"Maybe. I'll tell you one thing, though, this neighborhood isn't getting any better." The narrow street was a jumble of poor houses. None of them showed a light at that midnight hour, and passers-by were few. Nels and Oscar stayed on the opposite side of the street, walking as quietly as they could, hoping no one would glance back. Up ahead, Corny and the girl turned in through an archway and disappeared.

"Duck down behind this car!" said Oscar, anticipating that the two men, if they actually were up to no good, would glance back to check the street before jumping Corny. Crouching, they watched through the windows of the parked car that was shielding them. The men looked over their shoulders and then darted in through the archway.

"Come on, Nels!" The boys crossed over and raced up the street. The archway led into a small, dirty courtyard.

When they reached it they heard sounds of a scuffle.

Corny was proving a lively victim. Both men had jumped him and one had a hand over his mouth. The other had a blackjack poised, waiting for a chance to use it. Nels dived for him and knocked it out of his hand. Beside him Oscar came in swinging.

It was close work, a confusing whirl of flying fists and kicking feet. Nels felt his fist land solidly with a force that brought forth a satisfying grunt, and then the two thugs scrambled free. Now that the odds had changed, their only thought was to escape. They raced through the archway like two gray rats and pounded off down the street.

The girl had vanished. Corny was sitting on the cobblestones of the courtyard massaging his face. Rather than waste their time chasing the thugs, Nels and Oscar turned back to him.

"Well, anyway, I got in one good lick," said Nels, inspecting the bleeding knuckles of his right hand. "Somebody's going to have a beautiful shiner tomorrow."

"Quite so, Lord Nelson. He sure is," agreed Corny, taking his hand away from his left eye, which was rapidly closing.

"Cripes!" gasped Nels. "Was that *you* I hit?"

"I guess so." Naturally enough, Corny seemed deeply embarrassed by the discovery that one of his rescuers was Nels, but he managed to rise above his feelings. "Thanks for the assist, anyway, men — I'd have been in worse shape without you. Where the devil did you come from?"

Oscar explained.

"I see. That no-good, sneaky, two-faced — wasn't she a doll, though?" Corny shook his head with a sad grin. He rose and dusted himself off. Oscar located his cap for him. "So sweet and nice, too. When she asked me to take her home I was really excited. I guess she got a peek at my roll when I took out my wallet — I'm carrying more cash than I ought to be. Well, are you guys all right?"

"They never touched me," said Oscar.

175

"I'm okay, except my hand," said Nels, wrapping a handkerchief around his knuckles.

At one and the same instant the monstrousness of their situation dawned on Nels and Corny alike. They stared at each other, and Corny groaned.

"Oh, Judas! Now we've had it. What's going to happen when Mr. Jackson sees me with a black eye and you with skinned knuckles?"

Nels gulped. There was little doubt what would happen. Disaster of the darkest sort was staring them straight in the face. Mr. Jackson had been chillingly specific in his warning against fighting. His exact words still burned in Nels's mind — as though he had heard them only yesterday: "If either of you shows up back at this ship with a marked-up face or any other sign there's been a fight, it'll be the last time you ever fight as midshipmen. I'll fry you right out of the Academy." Nels's heart felt like a fifty-pound anchor as he remembered the stony look in Mr. Jackson's eyes at that moment.

"You're right," he agreed. "He's certainly not going to believe us if we tell him I hit you by accident. He'll think we're just trying to cover up."

"Of course he will. I would myself."

"Well," said Oscar, "maybe if I testified —"

"No, it still wouldn't be enough. Man, oh, man! We've really had it this time." Corny leaned weakly against the wall and screwed his good eye shut in frowning concentration. "No, no. We've got to keep cool here and think fast. We've got to think of ways and means."

176

"I wish that steak thing really worked on a black eye," muttered Nels.

"Well, it doesn't. No, we've got to . . ." Corny's good eye opened wide, and displayed a ray of hope. "Wait a minute. An alibi. That's what we've got to have, an alibi. And I think I know how to work it."

He outlined a plan.

"But you'll still get in trouble!" protested Nels. He was amazed to find himself worrying about Corny Schultz's hide, but they were in the same boat together now, and that made a difference.

"Okay, but it won't be anything like the trouble we'll both be in otherwise," Corny pointed out. "Go on, get going. I'll give you a good head start, because if anyone we know should see us together now the jig would really be up."

Nels and Oscar hurried back in the direction they had come, until they found the little cabaret Corny had named, the one in which he had met the girl. They posted themselves across the street from it and looked back to see if Corny was coming.

"There he is. He's stopping on the corner. Now, where's the shore patrol?"

They watched anxiously for the familiar white nightsticks and SP brassards, or armbands, of the Navy's own military police.

"When you want the guys they never show up."

"Yes, and our time's getting short. We ought to be

grabbing a taxi and high-tailing it back to the ship any minute now."

"You go ahead, Oscar. This isn't your problem."

"Nothing doing. You know how curious I am. Why, wild horses couldn't drag me away."

"But Oscar, you've got a good record. Don't risk it."

"Listen, there's such a thing as worrying too much about your record, ol' buddy. It can make a stuffed shirt out of a feller."

"Oscar, you're crazy to —"

"Never mind. Here they come!"

A pair of shore patrolmen hove into sight far up the street.

"Good!" Nels signaled Corny. The upperclassman walked to the cabaret and went inside. "About one minute after I walk in there, a hell of a row is going to start," he had predicted, and he made good on his prediction. Even out in the street Nels and Oscar could hear Corny's bellow raised over a babble of angry German voices.

"I tell you she tried to roll me! What kind of raunchy joint are you running here, you crooks, you? Come on, I'll lick anybody in the house!"

A little more of this, and Corny Schultz came back out of the cabaret, propelled by two worried-looking waiters in rumpled evening clothes who were trying to eject him as gently as possible.

"Please, go away. Go back to your ship, please!" they were saying. "Don't make trouble here, please."

"Let go of me," ordered Corny, flailing his arms about. "I'm going back in there and take the dump apart."

The approaching shore patrolmen had sighted trouble ahead now and were hustling to the scene. They pushed through the crowd that was gathering on the sidewalk.

"What's the trouble here?"

"A dame I met in there tried to roll me! That's the kind of dive it is!" Corny told them furiously. "I'm going to tear it apart."

"Please, take him away, please, *ja*, please?" said one of the waiters, delighted to see badges of authority appear on the scene.

"Come on, fellow, let's go."

"Let me alone! I'm going back in there!"

"You're not going anywhere except back to your ship," said one patrolman firmly, while across the street two midshipmen third class, who had seen and heard enough, eased away through the crowd and hailed a taxi.

"He did that real well," declared Oscar, as they sat back in their seats. "Say what you will, the guy has merit."

Nels examined his knuckles and sighed.

"For months on end I've dreamed of busting him one, and now that I have I can't even enjoy it!"

"What's this I hear, sir?" asked Nels when he reported to Corny next morning. "The fellows are saying you got into a row in some dive and the shore patrol had to bring you back to the ship."

"I had a little difficulty, yes, Crane, but it's nothing I'd care to discuss with an underling."

"Aye aye, sir. Incidentally, that's quite a shiner you have there, sir. You must have forgotten to duck."

"I was the victim of a cowardly assault, Crane. I was set upon by four thugs, and it took everything I had to beat them off."

"Bully for you, sir. Has Mr. Jackson had anything to say about it?"

"He questioned me briefly, chewed me out thoroughly, and will take the matter up further at mast. But all this has nothing to do with your work, Crane. Now, just what is the state of your cruise journal as of this minute? . . ."

# CHAPTER XIV

THE LONG-DREADED DAY had arrived. Mr. Jackson was holding mast.

All offenses that had accumulated during the cruise to that date, plus a few last-minute infractions at the Academy, were to be dealt with and suitable punishments meted out.

The maximum Mr. Jackson could give for a single offense was fifteen and four — fifteen demerits and four hours' extra duty. Nels knew he would receive the maximum for his spud locker offense, and at least ten and two on Lieutenant Sticky Stickney's charge of having his arm around Eloise on the steps of Bancroft Hall.

One appearance at mast would not have been so bad, but with two appearances and two penalties on his record he would have less chance than ever of finishing in the top quarter among his class on the cruise — and with each day his determination to make a good showing, and at least give his father that satisfaction, had increased. He was working hard, but even hard work could not wipe out two such marks on his record. The best he could hope for was to finish somewhere in the middle. Mediocrity! It was not much to be able to offer his father.

Mast was held in the after wardroom. Waiting on deck outside was a grim experience, because the hatchway was open and some of what was said inside could be heard by those whose turn was yet to come. Mr. Jackson's voice rasped through the air like a whine of a buzz saw, and "fifteen and four" was heard with depressing regularity. For reading a "skin book" on watch (a twenty-five-cent paper book with lots of feminine skin on its cover), fifteen and four. "Do you think you would sleep well if you knew that while you were in the rack everyone on the bridge from the OOD on down was readin' a book? To help you remember that bridge watch is one of the most important duties a man can have in a ship, I'm givin' you fifteen and four." For returning to the ship full of beer and using one of the awnings stretched above the after deck as a hammock, fifteen and four. "And the only reason I'm not givin' you more is because I can't!" For making a belt on watch in the engine room, fifteen and four. "A watch is no place for handcrafts."

When the belt-maker had reappeared and shambled away, the midshipman master-at-arms beckoned to Nels.

"Crane."

Nels took a deep, shaky breath, squared his shoulders, and followed him inside. Behind Nels came the midshipman who was his current division officer in the Engineering phase. This officer was the offender's closest approach to a defense attorney, and even he could not defend him against the charges, but only perform the role of a sort of character witness by reporting on the quality of work the man had been doing aboard ship.

Flanked by the master-at-arms and his division officer, Nels stood at attention before the desk, uncovered, and reported.

"Midshipman Crane, third class, sir."

Behind the desk, standing, were Mr. Jackson and his assistant. At one side stood the midshipman executive officer.

The exec handed the slip giving the charge to Mr. Jackson, who read it aloud.

"Mr. Crane, on June seventh you were placed on report for being absent from duty without leave — specifically, being found hidin' half-asleep in the spud locker by Mr. O'Leary. Have anything to say for yourself?"

Nels could feel his cheeks grow hot, and knew his face must be red.

"No excuse, sir." Regardless of Corny Schultz's part in getting him there, he felt he could offer no defense. Staying in the locker had been his own idea. Eyes front, chin back, Nels waited for the ax to fall. As was his way, Mr. Jackson let his eyes bore into the midshipman for a long, silent moment. When he spoke, it was to the division officer.

"How's this man's work, Mr. Morgan?"

"Excellent, sir. He's been one of my best men."

Mr. Jackson's eyes returned to Nels.

"Mr. Crane, you remember what I said at the time of

183

this offense about the kind of showing you were making on the cruise?"

"Yes, sir."

"You've come a long way since then. I don't think any man has shown more improvement than you have since that time. Takin' that into consideration, I'm not going to give you fifteen and four, which I probably should. I'm makin' it ten and two."

Nels blinked. He was so surprised that it took a nudge to remind him the ceremony was over.

"Thank you, sir." He covered, saluted, and went outside to await his second appearance. He could scarcely believe what had happened. Could this be Mr. Jackson? Could this be the Navy?

"Nice going, Nels," murmured another third classman in the waiting group. He looked envious, but he grinned as he added, "Why didn't anyone ever tell me hard work pays off in this outfit?"

"I'm as surprised as you are, Joe," Nels admitted. He was thrown off stride by this unexpected turn of events, but before he could really get his thoughts sorted out it was Corny Schultz's turn. Forgetting his own problems for the moment, Nels strained his ears to listen.

Mr. Jackson had a good deal to say on the subject of midshipmen conducting themselves properly in foreign ports. He also asked a number of pertinent questions.

"Mr. Schultz, do you consider that it adds to the dignity of the United States Navy for a midshipman to start a brawl in a cabaret and get tossed out with a black eye?"

"No, sir."

"Neither do I. Were you drunk?"

"No, sir."

*"H'm.* The shore patrol who returned you to the ship seemed to agree. They reported that you didn't appear to be drunk. What made you act that way, then?"

"I was angry, sir, because a girl I met in the place had tried to have me rolled. I felt the cabaret was partly to blame for letting a girl like that operate on the premises."

There was a moment of silence.

"You have quite a head of red hair, haven't you, Mr. Schultz?"

"Yes, sir."

"And a temper to go with it, right?"

"I'm afraid so, sir."

"Well, I think you'd better work on that temper, Mr. Schultz. You'd also better be a little more careful in your choice of female companions. And just to help you remember all these things, I'm going to give you fifteen and four. Do you think that'll help?"

"Yes, sir."

Nels had to force himself to look at the upperclassman when Schultz came out. A black eye, fifteen demerits, and four hours extra duty! In coming to Schultz's aid in that courtyard he had managed to make quite a mess of things.

A few minutes later Nels was back in the wardroom again to face his second charge.

"Well, Mr. Crane. This is a busy day for you, isn't it? Let's see, now, what is it this time? Oh, yes. You allegedly had your arm around a young lady on the steps of Bancroft Hall, right?"

"Yes, sir."

"Let's see, who was it caught you? Oh, yes — Lieutenant Stickney. *H'm*. Yes."

Strange things sometimes happen to stern Navy discipline at the mention of the fair sex. Being a bachelor, and a gay blade himself during off-duty hours, Mr. Jackson found it hard to treat such a charge as the present one with all the proper seriousness. He could do nothing at all about the fierce grin that slowly spread across his face, except to keep his voice perfectly steady and go on talking as though the grin were not there at all. But his grin made everyone else grin. Suddenly the room was full of sternly frowning, broadly grinning men, each struggling steadfastly to act as though nobody were grinning, least of all himself.

"Did you have your arm around the young lady, Mr. Crane?"

"Yes, sir. But not when I was written up, sir."

"Oh, no?"

"What I mean is, I don't think Mr. Stickney actually saw me, sir."

"You don't?"

"No, sir."

"You mean, you didn't have your arm around the young lady when he came along?"

"No, sir, not at the time I was put on report. What I mean is, Mr. Stickney was not personally present at any

186

time when it might have been charged that I had my arm around the young lady, sir."

"Oh. You mean, he was at some distance from you at the time when it could have been charged that you had an arm around the young lady, is that it?"

"Yes, sir. In fact, it must have been quite a distance, sir. I looked around right away afterwards and didn't see him anywhere in sight."

A general snicker slipped loose and was quickly suppressed.

"I see. That was prudent of you, Mr. Crane." Mr. Jackson coughed, and studied the slip in his hand. "Unfortunately, Mr. Stickney doesn't clarify his charges here. He doesn't indicate whether they're based on firsthand observation or secondhand information or thirdhand gossip or what. Makes it difficult to judge. As I remember that last day at the Academy, everything was in a mess. Lots of confusion. Poor visibility, even. It was rainin', and the steps were probably slippery. It may well be that you were only helpin' the young lady down the steps, steadyin' her to keep her from fallin'." Mr. Jackson stood tapping his thumbnail with the slip of paper, while they all shared a moment of silent thought about Sticky Stickney. "All in all, I don't think there's much of a case here. So I'm goin' to dismiss the charges."

When Nels had departed, trying to digest the incredible fact that he had come out of it all with a total of only ten and two, the next case brought forth further grins. This time the charge was more serious — kissing a girl in Bancroft Hall — and there was one big difference in the case: the man involved had been caught in the act. Mr. Jackson gave him ten and two, and a piece of good advice.

"Next time," said the lieutenant, "don't get caught."

Relaxing in his bunk, Nels thought his troubles were over for the day, until one of his classmates brought him a disturbing message.

"Mr. Jackson wants to see you again," he reported ominously. "Better lay up to the after wardroom on the double."

When he got there Nels found a shock in store for him. His heartbeat skipped unpleasantly as he stepped into the room and found only two other men there: Mr. Jackson, sitting in stony silence behind the desk; and Corny Schultz, standing frozen at attention in front of him.

Nels fell in alongside Corny. They stood immobile, moving not a muscle, eyes straight ahead. Mr. Jackson said nothing. He simply sat and looked at them, while the silence grew more and more oppressive, and its significance more and more inescapable. A question hung in the air between them as though it were burning there in letters of fire.

It was the upperclassman, as was fitting and proper, who finally broke the silence.

"Yes, sir, you're right about the black eye, but it was an accident, sir. And it was such a crazy accident we knew that you couldn't be expected to believe our story, especially after the warning you gave us about fighting. But I repeat, sir, we weren't fighting. We were fighting together. I mean on the same side. Well — to begin at the beginning . . ."

Throughout the story, as Corny recounted the events of that evening in Hamburg, Mr. Jackson's expression never changed. And when Corny finished, there was a long, long silence during which both midshipmen endured the slow, creeping trickle of tiny beads of sweat. When Mr. Jackson finally stirred and sat forward, they both jumped in spite of everything that military discipline could do for them.

"All right," said Mr. Jackson, and his jaw had a bulldog thrust to it. "I just didn't want you to think you were foolin' anybody around here. Dismissed."

And that was all he ever had to say on the subject.

Replenishing at sea from a supply ship took place only once during the cruise, en route to Cuba. The "reefer," as the men called such ships, was a tubby freighter with a tendency to yaw in a heavy sea, and a fair sea was running the morning the *Morton* went alongside to replenish.

The *Hyades* had two or three sets of cranes, but they did not enter into operations at sea other than to lift stores around on deck. The *Morton's* stores were piled on deck, waiting for her, when she came alongside, and were high-lined over in cargo nets.

While waves reached for the nets and rushed like rowdies up the sides of the ships, the supplies were hauled across and set down on the O-1 deck. A heavy roll sent a case of oranges over the side before anyone could reach it.

"Always lose some stuff when the sea's kicking up," a white hat told Nels.

A few other crates were broken open in handling, not always by accident. Somehow at least one crate of oranges and another of apples never managed to reach the storeroom on these occasions. Somehow they flew open, and everybody grabbed. Grabbed and passed, for sailors were good about taking care of their shipmates. In fact, the whole operation was a source of wonder to one of the officers on the bridge.

"What I can't figure out is how the stuff gets around so quickly," he remarked. "Look — even the *helmsman* is eating an orange!"

Meat, frozen vegetables, butter, milk — things that needed refrigeration — were chained down from the O-1 level to the forward fanroom, down the ladder, around the bend, down another ladder into the midshipmen's forward sleeping compartment, and then down one more level to the refrigeration rooms, deep in the bow of the ship. Some of the boxes, such as boxes of frozen turkeys and pork loins, were large and heavy, a tight fit to get down through the narrow spaces. Everybody worked, and worked hard, chaining them down. The physical workout, the speed, the teamwork made the job a welcome change from the usual routine. Replenishing was done briskly and with spirit.

The *Morton* did not get all that Mr. O'Leary had ordered, however: fifteen hundred pounds of beef failed to show up. Mr. O'Leary hit the overhead. He was shook. The situation was hairy. The *Morton* faced a menu of baked ham, boiled ham, ham croquettes, ham hash, frizzled ham, and minced ham, with chicken, turkey, and hot dogs as the only variety.

Mr. O'Leary took the trail with his characteristic energy and ran down the missing beef. It had been given to the *Weekes* by mistake. They would pass it over at the first opportunity.

"Oh, great! Now we'll get fifteen hundred pounds of the worst cuts," he prophesied gloomily. "We'll never get back our own meat."

Nor could anybody ever convince him that they did.

Nels came down the ladder into the forward engine room practically on the heels of Corny Schultz.

"Well, well! And what do we owe this honor to?" asked Chief Kane. "You guys got the midwatch?"

"We've got some extra duty to work off," Corny explained.

"Yeah? Hey, guys, here's the cake boys! Bring chairs! Shorty, fix a couple of mugs of jo!" Kane was only having fun, but nevertheless their stock was still high in the engine room.

"Make that one chair and a handful of rags, Chief," said Corny. "Only first classmen are going to loaf on this watch."

"Here's java. Cream and sugar here if you want it," said Shorty. They thanked him and doctored their coffee to taste.

"Listen, Mr. Schultz, I wouldn't blame you for being pretty sore about this extra duty," said Nels.

Corny took a sip of his coffee, staring with level eyes across the top of the mug at Nels. Then he lowered it and nodded, as though acknowledging the truth of his own thoughts.

"Crane, you've improved," he said bluntly. "A while back you'd have looked at things differently. You'd have gone out of your way to remind me that I ought to be grateful to you for pulling those two goons off my back."

It was a left-handed compliment that took Nels by surprise. It also surprised him into the realization that what Corny said was true. A month earlier he would have reacted exactly the way Corny described.

Life had become doubly confusing, because so many things and persons seemed to have changed. Oscar Tomlinson, Mr. Jackson, Corny Schultz — none of them had stayed put in the convenient niches he had assigned them at the beginning of the trip: eager beaver pest, Annapolis martinet, and sadistic bully. So much had changed — but it had never occurred to Nels until then that perhaps he had changed some himself.

"Besides, I'm not sore," Corny added. "We pretty well evened the score, I'd say. My stunt got you trapped in the spud locker and cost you ten and two. The black eye you gave me cost me fifteen and four."

"I owe you five demerits and two hours."

"I'll write off the demerits, and think of something to have you do with the two hours." Corny chuckled, and his fierce red eyebrows arched in triumph. "Just the same, we pulled it off pretty nice. If only Jackson didn't have a sixth sense about these things! . . . Well, you know why he has? Because he probably pulled every trick in the book himself when he was a midshipman."

"I'll bet he did, at that."

"Oh, well. We could do a lot worse than spend a few extra hours with our buddies here in the engine room, where we're treated like kings." Corny sat down in his chair and leaned back, sipping his coffee luxuriously. "Yes, sir. I can't complain. Okay, now, grab a rag and start wiping those pipes, Crane. There's nothing I like better than to take my ease and watch you work."

"Aye aye, sir!"

# CHAPTER XV

ONCE AGAIN the midshipman cruise settled into the routine of fifteen days at sea. The voyage from Europe to the southeastern tip of Cuba was generally considered the hardest and dullest stretch of the cruise. Despite the change of duties and classes as they entered Phase III of their training, much of what the midshipmen did now consisted of things they had already done before during the earlier parts of the cruise.

They had turned to again and again, every three or four days, to refuel. They had highlined an endless amount of guard mail, sometimes delivering it from ship to ship throughout the fleet. The drills had become repetitious, and the cruise journal assignments seemed ever a greater chore.

All work grew more difficult, too, because the weather turned steadily warmer as the fleet moved into southern waters. In the engine room, water injection showed a steady rise in the temperature of the sea, to seventy, seventy-four, seventy-eight degrees.

For those, like Nels and Oscar, who sat out on deck in the evenings and appreciated them, the night hours made up for everything. Night after night they sat on the fo'c'sle shooting the breeze with the deck force and watching Bangs do marvelous things with rope.

Calm, balmy, moonlit, the nights were too splendid to spend watching run-of-the-mill movies on the fantail — for now the evening show had moved out of doors, too. With the screen hanging from the twin barrels of Mount 53, and a big moon and bright stars shining overhead while soft breezes caressed their faces, the men of the *Morton* saw their movies in solid comfort and enjoyed all the advantages of a Caribbean cruise with one important exception. Oscar spoke about it one night while they lingered on the bridge, watching the ship slide smoothly through a glassy sea.

"A hunk of moon like that, and not one female within a thousand miles. I wonder if I'll ever see that Oola again?"

"I don't know, but I sure wish Eloise were here," declared Nels. Now that the ship was pointed back toward home and Eloise, Nels's fondest thoughts were pointed that way, too. "What a night! Wouldn't it be something to stand at the rail on a night like this with the right girl?"

Came a message from the engine room. "Request permission to blow tubes."

The OOD cast an eye up to check wind direction, and found it suitable — a cross-wind that would carry most of the soot clear of the afterdeck.

"Permission granted."

The stacks roared and hissed, and clouds of black soot filled the air. Oscar snorted in disgust.

"That engine room! No romance!"

There were a few special events during those weeks. For Nels and Oscar, Phase III was gunnery, and along with drills on the practice loading machines and tracking exercises in the gun mounts they did a good deal of actual firing. Sometimes they fired at a sleeve towed by a plane sent out from Bermuda, and sometimes at a pilotless drone operated from one of the battleships.

On one occasion the fleet drew up into columns, and a division of destroyers operating between the columns demonstrated the setting of various patterns of depth charges. Another time, at night, two widely separated columns took turns firing star shells over each other to demonstrate how effective these bright flares were in illuminating and silhouetting ships.

The time ahead seemed long, and yet each day passed in a flash. And though some of the midshipmen yawned and bitched and talked themselves into boredom, others made the most of their days at sea. Oscar's quiet interest in everything never flagged.

"Every place I look, there's still something I don't know," he said, "but these white hats are sure mighty patient with my questions."

Sailors are always looking ahead to the next port, of course. The sense of destination is ever important. Hence, among white hats and midshipmen alike, there was considerable talk and speculation about Guantánamo Bay.

From an operational standpoint, for the midshipmen, Gitmo promised to be eventful. They were to spend part of a day on submarines, and part of another day firing for the first time at a surface target — in this case, a water sled towed by a small auxiliary ship.

Most of the discussions, though, centered around the question of what they would and would not find when they hit the beach.

"Well, you sure won't find girls there," declared one upperclassman, speaking from the experience of his own youngster cruise two years earlier. "Gitmo's nothing but a big naval base, and the nearest town is off limits. Oh, a few Cuban girls come to a dance at the Officers' Club, but they always have their duennas along. You know what a duenna is. She's an old lady who comes along to make sure the girl doesn't duenna-thing."

"The food and the beer are cheap, though, and there's some good bargains at the PX," said another. "So all you can do is buy alligator bags and sixteen-jewel watches and stuff your face. Or play nice wholesome outdoor games, like baseball and tennis and golf. There's all kinds of recreational stuff, and plenty of swimming pools. Everything a good clean young American boy is supposed to need to keep his mind off women — only who wants to have his mind kept off women?"

If a plane had passed overhead one fine afternoon at about 67° W. 30° N., its passengers would have seen sixteen destroyers, dotted about over a wide area of ocean, going around in circles like so many whirligig waterbugs.

*"Moor on box drill"* was the order of the day, an ex-

cellent practical drill sometimes also called "rubber dock drill." The first classmen in gunnery were assembled on the bridge to take turns at having the conn. An empty orange crate was tossed into the water. The ship was taken out in a wide circle and brought back to the box, the idea being to approach it as though it were a mooring buoy, laying the ship's bow as close to it as possible.

Starting with the ship dead in the water alongside the box, the midshipman's first commands were, *"All engines ahead one third . . . All engines ahead two thirds . . . All engines ahead full."* Then, as soon as the ship had sufficient way to answer to its rudder, *"Left full rudder,"* or *"Right,"* as the case might be.

Presently, to widen the circle a bit and keep the box inside it, *"Rudder amidships"* for a moment or so. Then *"Left full rudder"* again, and a look through the pelorus to get a bearing on the box.

*"Bearing one six zero,"* said Corny Schultz, during his turn at the conn.

In the meantime, the helmsman was calling off the points of the compass as the ship turned.

"Passing two one zero . . . Passing two zero zero . . . Passing one nine zero . . . Passing one eight zero . . ."

*"Steady on one six zero."*

"Steady on one six zero."

"Very well."

The midshipmen's most frequent mistake was in not starting to stop soon enough. The exercise brought home to them the fact that a three-hundred-and-ninety-foot warship has a great deal of momentum when under way. The first few men overshot the mark badly. Keeping his binoculars steadily on the box, Corny barked out his next commands in good time.

*"All engines stop. Left full rudder."*

The ship slid on toward the box, bending in toward it slightly.

*"All engines back one third . . . All engines back two thirds . . . Starboard engine back one third . . ."*

The ship now was scarcely moving, and the box was almost alongside the port bow.

*"Rudder amidships. All engines stop,"* said Corny, and, having achieved a good approach, turned the conn over to the next man with the information, "All engines stopped, rudder amidships."

When all the midshipmen had taken turns at the conn, Captain Penn turned to Mr. Jackson.

"Mr. Jackson, would you care to take her around once?"

"Thank you, Captain, I certainly would," said the lieutenant, stepping forward with pleasure.

"Show us how, sir," called one midshipman.

"Just pay attention, then," replied their guide and mentor as he accepted the binoculars.

In the meantime, with the advance knowledge and full approval of the captain, word had been quietly passed down to the engine room that Mr. Jackson had the conn. It was not usual for the engine room to be informed as to who had the conn, but this was a special case.

Mr. Jackson got the ship under way, circled smartly, and gave the order, *"All engines stop."*

The order was transmitted to the engine room.

"Okay, leave on ten turns," suggested Chief Kane.

On the bridge Mr. Jackson frowned and gave his next order sooner than he had planned.

*"All engines back one third."*

"Okay, all engines stop and then back a few turns," said Kane down in the engine room, when the signal came through.

Mr. Jackson's frown deepened. The ship was certainly not answering properly, and the box was getting much too close much too soon.

*"All engines back two thirds!"* he roared.

"All engines back one third," suggested Chief Kane below.

With Mr. Jackson growing apoplectic on the bridge, the *Morton* went shooting past the box. The skipper glanced around and shook his head gently.

*"Tsk, tsk.* Mr. Jackson, I'm afraid you're rusty."

Not everybody on the bridge, as the badgered lieutenant whirled his gaze around, was able to hold his face as straight as the captain's. Sudden understanding flashed into Mr. Jackson's eyes.

"I've been had!" he cried, and everywhere within sight happy midshipmen began pounding each other on the back.

Indeed, throughout that golden afternoon it was touching to see how much fun a bunch of grown men could have with a couple of simple toys such as an old wooden orange crate and a twenty-million-dollar destroyer.

Alongside the spud locker a portside passageway ran inside the ship. Off this passageway, inboard, a door opened into a square room that always contained the same semidarkness, day and night. This was CIC, Combat Intelligence Center, also called simply Combat. This was the nerve center of the ship.

Here in Combat, spotted in various parts of a room not more than fifteen feet square, were speakers connected to several circuits — to the division and squadron flagships, to the flagship of the fleet (the battleship *Iowa*), and so on.

Here also were the radarscopes for air search and surface search, with their thin green radial lines endlessly sweeping circles around the black dials.

Nearby, the concentric circles of a maneuvering board showed through a table's glass top and through a large sheet of paper taped over the glass. The maneuvering board, which moved under the glass on the same course and relative speed as the ship, was called the "bug." On this board the positions of the entire fleet could be plotted, and from calculations made on it recommendations for course and speed were telephoned to the bridge during maneuvers.

Occasionally the radarman on the air search would announce, "Hey, I got a bogey on my screen." A blip had shown up on his scope that appeared to be a bogey — an unidentified aircraft. This would be reported to the bridge, and when the plane came in sight it usually proved to be a commercial airliner on a transatlantic flight.

Now and then, in the evening, Nels and Oscar looked in on CIC, particularly during message drills. One night they were privileged to listen to the fleet's only underground radio station.

When they entered the darkened room, a speaker in the corner nearest the maneuvering-board table rasped and crackled.

*"Swizzlestick, this is Wagonwheel. Swizzlestick, this is Wagonwheel. Over."*

"Wagonwheel, this is Swizzlestick. Over," replied a man wearing a headset.

The CIC officer, Mr. Buck, who was bending over the board, lifted his head to listen to the message. In Combat there were men who could scarcely recall at an instant's notice the actual names of the destroyers in the division, so accustomed were they to thinking of them by their code names. Wagonwheel for the *Weekes,* Bowhook for the *Lawrence,* and Headache for the *Wareham.*

When the message was finished Mr. Buck nodded, and the talker said, *"Swizzlestick. We concur. Out."*

*"Wagonwheel. Roger and out."*

*"Phantom. Roger and out,"* said a new voice, and everyone in Combat grinned.

"There he goes again."

"That character. He's gonna end up in the brig!"

"Ah, they'll never find him."

The Phantom was one of the fleet's prize examples of

202

midshipman humor. Somewhere, on one of the ships, someone had access to a circuit and was using it to add his own comments to the nightly radio message drills. When a drill was not going well, the Phantom was likely to pop onto the circuit with some such lugubrious message as, *"This is Phantom. The situation is deteriorating. Over and out."*

A new voice came on the circuit now, a crisp voice of authority, a voice that had had enough nonsense. It came from one of the heavies, which was conducting the drill.

*"This is Lightpost. All unauthorized messages on this frequency must cease. Do you concur?"* it added threateningly. *"Over."*

*"This is Wagonwheel. We concur."*

The *Morton's* talker pressed his button. *"This is Swizzlestick. We concur."*

The others chimed in.

*"This is Headache. We concur."*

*"This is Bowhook. We concur."*

*"This is Phantom. Do not concur,"* said the unauthorized voice.

Wherever the Phantom was operating from, his secret was well kept. He was never trapped.


Among the men aboard the *Morton* there was one in particular who was looking forward eagerly to Gitmo's extensive tennis courts and baseball diamonds.

Though primarily CIC officer, Mr. Buck numbered among his many subsidiary duties that of athletics officer. Mr. Buck was the *Morton's* "bull ensign," as the senior ensign is called. He had been aboard for nearly two years. Roly-poly of figure, with a round, heavy-jawed face that gave little indication of the keen mind behind it, he was a smart and capable young officer.

Where athletics were concerned, his special passion was baseball, and it was shared by as ragtag a group of some fifteen white hats as ever had the nerve to call themselves a baseball team. They possessed little equipment, not much talent, and no uniforms, but they did have one thing, and that was the strutting cockiness of destroyermen. They were ready to take on anybody.

Fired by this spirit, and filled with it himself, Mr. Buck put the signalmen to work one night on the bridge. Their blinkers sent out challenges to every heavy in the fleet for a baseball game at Gitmo. He even sent one to the lordly *Iowa,* home of the current Alantic Fleet champions, whose team had mopped up everyone in sight and made life miserable everywhere.

"I don't suppose any of them will stoop to playing a mere tin can," admitted Mr. Buck, "but it doesn't hurt to ask."

The *New Jersey* grandly ignored the challenge. The cruisers laughed it off as presumptuous. But the *Iowa,* having beaten everybody else, was desperate for new worlds to conquer. A little batting practice with some clowns from a rust-bucket was better than nothing. So . . .

"Men, we've got a game!" Mr. Buck announced, his round face betraying his utter amazement. "Get out on that deck and start limbering up your arms — we're playing the *Iowa!*"

# CHAPTER XVI

A**T** 0400 the midshipmen stumbled on deck, rubbing sleep out of their eyes, to find the ship entering Guantánamo Bay with dawn still to come. Hills stood out blackly against a sky of charcoal gray. From a high point near the water's edge a beacon light flashed, turning slowly. Moored on the edge of the channel was a shadowy hulk that looked like an enormous floating ranchhouse with a huge picture window, brilliantly lighted, in its side. As the *Morton* passed the towering mass the dim outlines of a bow beneath a broad platform made it more recognizable.

"It's a 'jeep' carrier," declared one middy, that being the name given to certain small aircraft carriers.

"It's a Limey carrier."

"No, I'll bet it's the *Leyte*."

"Naw! It's not that big."

"Well, you guys can argue, but I'm going to hit the chowline."

Breakfast was early that morning for the midshipmen. After fifteen days on the ocean, they were destined to put out to sea again before setting foot on land.

When the *Morton* and *Wareham* had nested alongside a fueling pier, their midshipmen crossed the pier and boarded waiting submarines. For the third classmen, and even for some of the first classmen, it was to be their first experience below the sea.

Low in the water like fat black needles, conning towers cut back like a shark's fin, even at rest the submarines had the sinister, lurking air of cloak-and-dagger assassins. They were savage hunters, and nothing could have made them look otherwise. Nor was it merely a suggestion of deadliness that they offered, for they were aging veterans of World War II, these submarines, and they knew all there was to know about war, violence, and death, except what it was like to be destroyed themselves. The one Nels and Oscar boarded had sunk twenty-two Japanese ships and damaged eight others.

The small open bridge of the submarine extended in front of the conning tower. From it the main hatch led down inside the tower, and there a second hatch led below into the hull of the ship. When the submarine was cruising on the surface and the captain was on the bridge, he gave his commands through the open main hatch to the helmsman standing at the wheel directly below him. With the captain was the diving officer. Lookouts stood on perches on each side of the bridge.

When it was time to submerge, the captain went below and took his post at the periscope, usually Number One periscope, looking forward. The last man to leave the bridge was the diving officer. When all was ready, he shouted the command, *"Clear the bridge! Clear the bridge!"*

What followed was action at breakneck speed. First the lookouts leaped down from their perches and dropped through the hatch into the conning tower without seeming to touch the rungs of the ladder, one man almost on top of the other. And all but stepping on the second man's neck came the diving officer, grabbing the cable that closed the hatch as he came. Setting his feet the minute he reached the conning tower deck, he put all his beef behind a tug-of-war pull on the cable to bang the main hatch shut and hold it while one of the men sprang back up the ladder and spun the wheel that closed the hatch tight.

*"Main hatch secured!"*

The jangling tones of a klaxon vibrated through the submarine, sounding twice — *"Ah-ooh-gah! Ah-ooh-gah!"* — the signal to submerge.

"Feel it in your ears?" asked Oscar. "Wouldn't know it otherwise, though — that we're going down, that is."

While the submarine cruised at periscope depth, with its keel sixty feet below the surface, which left the periscopes just above the level of the sea, the midshipmen were shown through the ship along the single central corridor that connected her various spaces such as the forward torpedo room, crew's mess, control room, officers' quarters, after torpedo room, and crew's quarters.

The submarine was no place for a Nervous Nellie who might object to living on cozy terms with high explosives. The crew's bunks hung directly over huge torpedoes, or "fish"; space was at a premium, and the extra fish had to be stored somewhere. On the other hand, the bunks' foam-rubber mattresses were excellent, much better than the mattresses aboard the destroyers.

"Why, a feller could sleep like a baby on one of these, as long as he didn't get to fretting about that big gadget underneath him there," commented Oscar.

The klaxon sounded three times, and the call, *"Surface, surface, surface!"* was heard.

The first dive was over.

A few more dives to periscope depth were made, and then, in order to acquaint the midshipmen with the sensation of making a really steep dive, the captain gave the command, *"Take her down to one hundred and fifty feet smartly."*

The deck slanted away under the soles of their shoes as the submarine plunged. They stood tipped back at a sharp angle, and this time there was no doubt as to what was happening. The men in the engine room were taking her down, and smartly, as the command specified. From distant parts of the submarine they could hear crashing and tinkling sounds, wherever small bits of gear had been left adrift. In the tiny officers' wardroom a silver drawer shot out of its slot and slid down the table, sweeping two coffee cups before it. Quick reflexes saved everything as two middies made a grab for them.

The hand of the depth indicator swept around the dial: 100 . . . 110 . . . 120 . . . 130 . . . At one hundred and fifty feet the ship leveled off smoothly.

When this special dive had been completed and the ship

had surfaced again, Nels heard one of the submarine officers make a strange remark to another.

"Well, I guess it's Nutty Buddy time now, huh?" he muttered.

Nels nudged Oscar.

"Hey, did you hear that?"

"What?"

"That officer said it's Nutty Buddy time. I wonder what he meant?"

The officer who had made the strange remark now faced the midshipmen with a warm smile on his lips. They were bunched together in the control room — thirty of them who had been brought aboard for the special trip. Rubbing his hands together like a genial host, the officer asked, "Well, now, who's ready for some refreshments?"

The midshipmen had eaten breakfast at 0430. It was now 1000. Nobody hung back when the officer led the way forward to the crew's mess.

There were just sufficient tables to allow all the middies to squeeze in at once. When they were seated, the submariners threw open a food locker concealed below the deck and began to show off.

One picture may be worth a thousand words, but sometimes one gallon of ice cream is worth a thousand pictures, and the submariners did not stop at a mere gallon. Out came the big round cartons, one after the other. Out came box after box of ice cream sandwiches and ice-cream bars frosted with milk chocolate covered with nuts. (These were the Nutty Buddies the officer had referred to.) Out came the cookies, and all the fresh milk they could drink.

The middies met the challenge manfully. Scooping quarts of ice cream into king-size bowls, they spooned it down in between devouring the Nutty Buddies they held in their free hands, and washed the whole down with glass after glass of milk. Their capacity would have amazed persons who had led sheltered lives ashore, away from centers of adolescent life. Aboard the submarine, however, it was taken for granted. There were no poor Herr Wieselgrens present to turn pale and burp at the sight.

"Did you ever see so much stuff in your life?" marveled Oscar.

"Vulgar display, that's what it is. Vulgar display," said Nels, picking another Nutty Buddy out of the box. "Pass the ice cream once more, will you, Oscar?"

When their guests had taken the first edge off their Gargantuan appetites and were munching contentedly, the officer who had issued the invitation pulled out a list of their names.

"Now, while you're here, fellows, we'd like to take a sort of poll to see how many of you are interested in the submarine service," he began smoothly. "Keep eating," he urged. "Just hold up a finger if you're interested when your name is called. Unless, of course, you're not interested, and then we'd like you to give your reason, or your other preference."

He paused to urge a midshipman who had only eaten three bowls of ice cream to have another. The midshipman did.

210

"Of course, as you probably already know," said the officer, turning to caress an outsized refrigerator in a suggestive way, "the icebox on a submarine is never locked, the way it is on other ships. Any man on this ship can come to the galley at any hour of the night or day, break out a steak and fry it for himself, if he feels hungry. . . . Well, now, to get on with our poll . . ."

He began to call off names, and one after another fingers began to go up, fingers belonging for the most part to men who had not even given submarines a thought until all that ice cream had started coming along. Oscar raised a finger, and so did Nels — after all, since it didn't matter anyway, there was no reason to hurt his host's feelings. Besides, if he *had* been going to stay in the Navy, he might have given some thought to a little submarine experience, at that.

Of course, a number of the midshipmen declared that they had their sights set on Navy Air. The submariners were ready for anything, however. When the poll had been completed, the officer even torpedoed the air arm with a few well-chosen words.

"I don't blame some of you for being attracted to naval aviation. Airplanes can be exciting. However, I wonder if you've really looked ahead, and kept in mind the fact that the whole air picture is changing rapidly and radically. Now, I don't want to knock another arm of the service, but I do want to point out the fact that you can't look forward to doing much flying."

He paused to let this shocking suggestion sink in, and then explained:

"I'm only being realistic. War planes are rapidly reaching the point where they will be beyond the capacities of human pilots. Guided missiles will soon take over completely, so far as air strikes are concerned. Some of you luckier ones may be able to get into the air as pilots of some lumbering boxcar of a transport, and be privileged to do a lot of ferry service, back and forth, back and forth, but most of you will be left in dull ground jobs."

His face had become sad as he presented this dismal picture, but now his expression brightened.

"On the other hand, let's take a look at submarines. Top men in the Navy agree that within sixty years 90 per cent of the fleet will be submersibles of some kind. Within your own naval careers, 60 per cent will be submersibles. So it's not merely the extra pay you should think about, even though it equals the flight pay you'll get — if you're lucky enough to fly at all, that is. It's not just the marvelous chow and the good living conditions with a small crew, and the special *esprit de corps* of the men who wear the dolphins on their chests, that you should think about, either. It's the future!"

It was a thoughtful group of midshipmen who filed out of the crew's mess. The submariners' propaganda mill had ground exceedingly well. As they filed past the wardroom the steward was setting the table for lunch, and, even there, there was food for thought.

"Did you get a look at that table?" asked one lad over his shoulder. "Their stuffed olives are *twice* the size of ours!"

There was bad news as far as mail was concerned. A batch of mail, including the *Morton's,* had been flown to London by mistake. Instead of being at Gitmo waiting for them, it was on its way back to New York. They would be lucky if they received it at all during their three-day stay in Cuba.

More and more, as the ship neared America, Nels's thoughts returned to Eloise. He had been living for the eight or ten letters he hoped to find waiting for him at Gitmo. The hold-up on the mail was a bitter disappointment.

"Just one more week now, ol' Nutty Buddy, and then she can sweet-talk you in person," Oscar pointed out.

"Yes, but I could use some letters in the meantime," said Nels. One more week! It didn't seem possible, but suddenly the time had narrowed to that exciting margin. One more week, and it would all be over. Over and in the past. He looked at Oscar. "You going to head for home as soon as we get ashore?"

"Quick as I can," nodded Oscar. "How about you?"

"Dad will be in Washington on business. He's going to drive over, see some old friends at the Academy, and take me on home with him."

"Man, think of it. A whole month's vacation!"

Nels looked away and said nothing. He wondered what Oscar would say if he knew that for him it would be the beginning of a permanent vacation from the Navy. Long ago, however, he had made up his mind that he would not tell Oscar about his decision during the cruise, nor dampen the pleasure of their homecoming by telling him at the last minute. He had Oscar's home address: he would write him about it later on. After their ways had parted, it wouldn't bother Oscar as much as it would now.

All day long the steel ships sat under the brazen sun of the tropics and soaked up heat, but even so Gitmo was not quite the inferno it had been painted. The evenings ashore were pleasant, and when they returned to the ship they could spread their mattresses on deck.

They shopped for bargains in the Post Exchanges with what little money they had left, and enjoyed the inexpensive food and beer the Navy clubs provided. They reveled in the swimming pools, and even attempted a few dances with some of the heavily escorted Cuban girls who came to the hops that were arranged for the midshipmen.

During duty hours aboard ship the midshipmen gun crews were receiving a concentrated dose of surface tracking exercises in preparation for the climax of all their work with the guns — firing practice at surface targets. After what they had thought was their final session of practice one morning, they received a message from Mr. Jackson.

"Your work isn't bad, it isn't terrible. It stinks. We'll do it again this afternoon."

There were the final cruise journal assignments to finish up, and "ladders" to be filled out. On these ladders — "aptitude worksheets," they were officially called — each midshipman had to rate his classmates according to his judgment of their capabilities, officer qualities, and the showing they had made on the cruise. Concerning the bottom 10 per cent, he had to write chits telling why he placed them at the bottom.

At the same time Mr. Jackson and his assistant were also filling out ladders, and on these and on the midshipmen's would be based the final standing of the men.

Among the third classmen there was little question as to who would be top grease man. Nobody had put more into the cruise and got more out of it than Oscar Tomlinson, and his work showed it. Nels remembered now with amazement his first reaction — a feeling of superiority — to his friend. The memory of the attitude with which he had started the cruise made his wistful hopes for a high rating seem presumptuous. He had tried hard, after a while, yes — but had the damage already been done?

Five thousand yards away, across the sparkling tropical blue sea, the sled moved through the water at the end of a long, long towing cable. The auxiliary ship doing the towing was a dot in the water far up ahead of the sled. Slowly the *Morton* closed the range, while inside the five-inch gun mounts the midshipmen crews waited tensely for the all-important command: *"Fire when ready."*

In Mount 52, Nels and Oscar stood poised beside the portside gun. Their lessons as projectile man and powder man had been learned. Oscar had learned to take the charge from the powder hoist and place it in the breech in one swift, continuous movement. Nels had learned to step

215

on the projectile lift release with his foot, grasp the heavy projectile, set it in place in front of the charge, and hit the rammer lever with his left hand all in far less time than it takes to tell. They had learned to keep their fingers clear and to make fists the instant they had let go of powder case and projectile. In that dangerous center of lethal machinery, where heavy pieces of steel mechanism moved with such brutal finality, they had learned to keep their arms and legs clear of breech and gun pit. And like everyone else in the mount — the pointer, the trainer, the other gun crew, the mount captain — they were thinking of nothing else but their determination to do everything that head and heart and muscle were capable of to make the best showing of any gun mount in the division.

The squawk box suddenly crackled with the voice of the gunnery officer from the main fire control director, above the bridge.

*"Mount 52, surface action to starboard. Surface action to starboard."*

*"Mount 52 in automatic."*

After a couple of kidney-shaking jerks the mount wheeled, training its guns to starboard and bringing them on target.

*"Stand by. . . . Fire when ready."*

Swift, concentrated effort. Powder case in place, projectile in place, the rammer lever hit. Powder and shell rammed home, the muffled roar of the blast, the rattle-snake-strike recoil of the gun, the rattle of empty brass as the hot case slid out through the case ejector port and hit the deck. Three shots gotten off; four, five, six . . .

"*Cease fire. Cease fire.*"

The sudden quiet.

"*Mount 52, shift to local and train centerline.*"

Slowly the mount swung back until its guns were pointing exactly forward, parallel with the centerline of the ship.

"*Mount 52 trained centerline,*" reported the mount captain, and grinned excitedly as he stuck his head down into the mount. "We were close every time, and I think we got at least two hits!"

One after another, the mounts took their turn. The shells whistled out toward the sled, seconds ticked past, and then at last, somewhere near the sled, a column of water shot into the air to mark where the shell had hit. Sometimes, at close range, when the ship moved in to three thousand yards, the shots skipped on the water, and sent up a second column of water a thousand yards farther out.

High up on top of the main fire control director, Mr. Jackson looked on and felt somewhat rewarded for the two months of watching and scolding and chewing-out he had put in. The boys were giving him a good shoot. As he pulled the cotton out of his ears, he permitted himself a brief nod of satisfaction.

"Not bad," he growled. "I guess there's some hope after all."

# CHAPTER XVII

Baseball equipment aboard the *Morton* consisted of a dozen gloves, half a dozen bats, and five old, scuffed baseballs. At least, there had been five baseballs when the "team," as it was laughingly called, began to limber up.

The only place where two men could throw a baseball back and forth on a tin can was along the narrow strips of deck that ran down each side of the ship. One wild throw, or one bad fumble, and the baseball was over the side, bobbing in the wake as the ship left it far behind.

For its pitcher the team had Bangs, an aging spitball artist who had once pitched for Deslant (Destroyers Atlantic Fleet) until he broke his arm. When the wild throws of various lesser lights had reduced the supply of baseballs by four, Mr. Buck announced that the remaining ball was to be reserved for Bangs's warm-up sessions.

The ship was still one day out of Gitmo when Bangs unloosed a wide one while warming up. The storekeeper split his thumb trying to hold it, the ball went over the side, and Bangs grabbed his shoulder in pain.

"I pulled something that time," he announced. A minute later he was in sick bay with his shirt off, sitting with his shoulder under a heat lamp while Doc inspected it anxiously. The little chief medical corpsman played center field himself, so his concern was unfeigned.

Mr. Buck was disconsolate.

"Now we're really in great shape. We haven't got a pitcher. My catcher's split his thumb. We haven't got uniforms. And we haven't got a single baseball. The guys have to warm up with oranges. Meanwhile those bums on the *Iowa* have probably got ten pitchers to choose from, and they've got a ship so big that in bad weather they could warm up belowdecks. How can we field a team? Why, there's only about fifteen guys on this can who even *think* they can play, and half of those are restricted to the ship, so that I'll be lucky if I can get them excused for the game."

The men in question had made recent appearances at captain's mast because of various offenses committed in port, and had been fined and given thirty or sixty days' restriction to the ship as punishment.

All in all, the odds, overwhelming to begin with, had become truly crushing. The pitching situation seemed hopeless.

"Hey, look, Mr. Buck," said Feeney. He and a cook named Michaels had found a hard green orange that was holding up pretty well as Michaels burned in a few fast pitches. "He gets a nice hop on that orange. Maybe he can pitch for us."

Mr. Buck watched glumly. He was not impressed.

"He may be pretty good with fruit, but those sluggers from the *Iowa* aren't going to be hitting oranges, Feeney, they're going to be hitting baseballs."

Imbued with the proper never-say-die spirit of the true destroyerman, however, Mr. Buck kept searching for ways and means, and for pitching talent. The game was scheduled for the final night of their four-day stay at Gitmo. Even if Bangs's shoulder had not loosened up, maybe by then he could uncover some other pitching talent.

The final insult was offered by the manager of the *Iowa's* team, a sawed-off gunner's mate who was called, inevitably enough, Shorty. As soon as they reached Gitmo, Mr. Buck met with Shorty to make final arrangements for the game. When he mentioned the fact that his best pitcher was having shoulder trouble, Shorty dared to offer him one of the *Iowa's* pitchers for the game. His was the patronizing manner of the Big Fellow helping out the Little Fellow. Its effect was as though he had waved a red flag in front of the bull ensign.

"No, thank you," said Mr. Buck in his chilliest voice. "And furthermore, we're going to tear your ears off!"

Shorty laughed indulgently.

"In a pig's eye, sir," he retorted.

Mr. Buck returned fuming to the *Morton*.

"The nerve of that guy, offering *us* a pitcher! Not that I know where we're going to get one, but we won't use one of theirs if I have to pitch myself!"

Fortunately, word of the game had passed around

among the division. Like manna from heaven, a message came to Mr. Buck from the *Weekes*. Soon after that he was able to make an important announcement.

"We've got a pitcher! There's a midshipman on the *Weekes* who pitched for the plebe team, with a ten and three record!"

From the *Wareham*, which had once had a ball team, came an offer of uniforms. Things were definitely looking up. With a ringer from the *Weekes* on the mound and uniforms from the *Wareham* on their backs, the team could almost feel it was representing the division in this David-and-Goliath encounter. And on the *Morton*, a few of the midshipmen — including Corny Schultz and Nels — were interested to hear that Mr. Buck would consider using midshipmen on the ship's team.

"Listen, I'll use the division commodore if he wants to play," said Mr. Buck. "Certainly I'll use you guys, if you can help us. What positions do you play?"

"I've worked behind the plate some," said Corny.

"Good. My catcher's thumb is healing pretty well, but I'd like to have you on hand just in case." Mr. Buck turned to Nels. "How about you?"

Every midshipman at Annapolis had to go out for some sport. Nels had chosen baseball.

"I usually play the outfield." He hesitated, and then, "I've also tried to pitch a little, but I'm not too hot on the mound."

"I see. Well, turn out just in case. Do you know anything about Carlson, this kid I got from the *Weekes?*"

221

"Yes, sir. He's good."

"I hope so. He'll have to be, to handle those murderers from the *Iowa*. All I hope is that we can at least make it interesting and go down fighting!"

It was the afternoon of the fleet's final day at Gitmo. Nels and Oscar were about to go ashore with two other third classmen for a doubles tennis match, when the motor whaleboat returned from a run loaded with mailbags.

They hung around eagerly, waiting for the mail to be sorted, and then bunched together for a midshipmen mail call.

It seemed to Nels as if his name would never be called. Oscar got two letters from home, and even a postcard from Claribel Hatch, but Nels had yet to score.

"I sure ought to hit the jackpot when I *do* get started," he declared.

"Crane!"

"Here!"

It was a letter from his brother, Perry. A moment later he jumped at the sound of his name again. This time he was handed a letter from his father.

"I don't understand it. Maybe this is only part of our mail," he decided.

Then, when the mail clerk was really scraping the bottom of the bag, his name was called once more, and he was handed a letter from Eloise.

"One letter! How do you like that? There must be a lot more mail somewhere."

"Well, maybe so, but come on, we've got to make tracks. The boat's ready to shove off. Let's take our mail to the club and read it in comfort over a nice cold beer."

Only the main clubhouse was denied to the third classmen at the officers' club. Everything else was at their disposal. The four third classmen from the *Morton* changed into tennis shorts in the bathhouse and then went out to sit at a table under the palm trees with a round of beers. They settled down to the luxury of reading their mail before beginning their tennis match.

Nels opened Eloise's letter first. He raised his beer can on high.

"Well, here's to the ladies, God bless —"

His beer can remained frozen in mid-air. His toast to the ladies was left unfinished. Nels read the brief letter at a glance and his face went white.

"Oscar."

Oscar looked up. Nels's expression startled him.

"What's the matter?"

"She's sent me a Dear John."

"What? You're kidding."

"No, I'm not. She's engaged to that Ronald jerk!"

He handed the letter to Oscar, and tried to absorb this sudden, stunning news. Just when he had put all other girls out of his mind, just when he had got back to thinking of no one but her, she had done a thing like this!

The other fellows were staring at him now, realizing what had happened. It was a humiliating situation to be in, to sit there and let them all see how bad he felt about having

223

some snake-in-the-grass grab his girl away from him. Nels tried to pull himself together and make a show of taking it more in stride. He tipped his chair back from the table and laughed a somewhat hollow laugh. His face felt stiff and twisted as he talked.

"Well, I guess that calls for a drink. A real drink. I guess I'll drown my sorrows. That's the thing to do, isn't it? Gee, this couldn't have come at a better time than here at Gitmo, where good liquor is only thirty cents a drink."

Oscar handed the letter back to him.

"Ol' buddy, I don't blame you. But this is an awful early hour to start drowning your sorrows. Why don't you whack the cover off a tennis ball for a while first? I know I'd feel like hitting something at a time like this if I were you."

"Nuts to tennis."

Nels glowered at his friend for a moment. Then he lifted his beer can again. "As I was saying, here's to the ladies, God bless 'em!"

He drained the can and set it down. "Okay, who's for tennis?"

"I am," said Oscar. "Come on — you and I can start warming up while these guys finish their letters."

As far as Nels was concerned, the tennis ball was Ronald. Every time he hit it, he saw Ronald as he imagined him to be. Wavy blond hair, worn too long. Small, shifty eyes set too close together. Nasty little mouth. Pockets full of money, and driving a long, sleek convertible.

"You must want to kill that Ronald feller," said Oscar. "You sure are killing the ball."

224

They played four sets of tennis. When they had finished, Oscar said, "Okay, Nels, I'll be right with you, just as soon as I've had a dip."

"A dip?"

"Well, that swimming pool looks mighty inviting."

Nels faltered. Now that Oscar mentioned it, the idea of a swim, after four sets of tennis, was tempting, even to a man whose heart had just been broken.

"Well, I guess I'll have a quick dunk, too," he decided grudgingly.

After their swim, Oscar declared he was hungry as a bear.

"I'm too hungry to enjoy any serious drinking yet, ol' buddy. If you don't mind waiting, I think I'll have a bite to eat first. Let me just stop in here at the snack bar and pick up a couple of steak sandwiches and some French fries."

In spite of the pain in his heart, Nels was unable to ignore the pain that Oscar's careless words had caused in his stomach. The thought of Eloise in the arms of that skunk with the flashy convertible (and probably a motorboat as well) might have made him wipe the corners of his eyes, had not the aroma of hamburgers and steaks frying on the griddle made him wipe the corners of his mouth instead.

"Maybe I'll have a little something, too," he decided. "Make that a double order."

While they were eating, Oscar had still another thought.

"Aren't you supposed to show up at the ball game to-night?"

Nels sat back and stared at his friend suspiciously.

"Oscar, it's mighty funny the way you keep coming up with one thing after another!"

"Why, what a thing to say, ol' buddy!"

"Don't give me that innocent look. And forget about the ball game. They don't need me. I'm a lousy pitcher anyway."

"Still, I think we ought to walk down to the ball field and just make sure Mr. Buck doesn't want you."

The trouble with Oscar's arguments was they were usually based on the sort of common sense that was hard to get around. By the time Nels had cleaned up the last of the French fries — his second order, that is — he felt better.

The lights were just coming on for the night games down at the big recreation field.

"Well, all right. But only for a couple of innings!"

# CHAPTER XVIII

**R**ESPLENDENT IN SPOTLESS UNIFORMS, the *Iowa's* team handled three easy chances with snap and precision as their pitcher mowed down the top of the *Morton's* order in the first inning.

The tin-can team then took the field in a set of uniforms that looked as if they had come straight from the ragbag of a needy family. The shirts were worn inside-out to hide the letters W A R E H A M on their chests. Bergen, the catcher, had his thumb taped, and Bangs, playing right field, had his shoulder strapped. Four members of the team were officially Mr. Buck's prisoners for the evening. About all their manager could say for the lot of them was that at least they were sober.

The first *Iowa* batter singled sharply to center. The next man hit an easy fly to left that Korowski, who wore glasses, lost in the lights. Both runners romped home. But then, when despair was hovering over *Morton* rooters like a vulture, Carlson settled down and struck out the side.

Not many rooters from either ship had bothered to come to the game, but the can's small contingent made a lot of noise. Nobody made more than Oscar. He was the *Morton's* most tireless rooter. There was plenty to make noise about, too, because in the bottom of the second inning the game exploded.

To begin with, Bangs walked, and the next man singled him to third. Then Korowski, still mad about dropping that easy fly, doubled to center — and brought them both home.

From that point on, the *Morton* men played like demons, and nothing seemed to go right for the *Iowa*. Three of her pitchers came and went, while the battlewagon's team specialized in throwing the ball away. By the top of the fifth, the *Morton* was leading 10 to 4 — and the game was only scheduled to go seven innings.

In the *Morton* dugout, every man was in a state of feverish excitement, giving his all as a bench jockey. Each time the *Iowa* team went to bat, its manager was in the third-base coach's box in front of his opponents' dugout, and unfortunately poor Shorty had rabbit ears.

"Hey, Shorty, do you still want to lend us a pitcher?" yelled Mr. Buck, after the third *Iowa* pitcher had been shelled from the mound. Shorty's shoulders hunched as though he had taken an arrow in the back.

"You wait, you'll need him yet," he retorted, but without much conviction. Carlson was mowing his boys down like a veteran.

"If we can only hold them!" muttered Mr. Buck in a

prayerful tone. "Can you imagine, a tin can knocking off the Atlantic champs? Why, every ship in the fleet will hear about it!"

It was too good to last, of course.

First Bergen's thumb opened up again and Corny Schultz had to go in to catch. In the bottom of the fifth the *Iowa* scored twice, and when Carlson came out he looked tired and worried.

"I haven't pitched since May, so my arm's not really in shape. It's beginning to tighten up on me, I'm afraid."

All along the bench, faces fell. The manager turned anxiously to Bangs.

"Can you go an inning?"

"Hell, no. My shoulder's stiff as a board. If they hit one out to me I'll have to carry it in."

Mr. Buck gulped. Then he grabbed a bag and dug a uniform out of it.

"Hey, Crane. Get into this."

Nels looked out at the *Iowa* players who were taking the field, and began to feel about ankle-high to a mouse. They would slaughter his stuff — because he really didn't have any.

"Come on, turn to!"

"Aye aye, sir." Nels began briskly to change clothes, with Oscar helping him. If there was nobody else, then he'd have to do the best he could.

The uniform fitted like a glove — a lefthanded glove. It was tight where it should have bagged, and it bagged where it shouldn't have. The tailor who, long ago, made the uniform had obviously had a much shorter and fatter man in mind.

"Okay, start warming up. Maxwell, you warm him up, and keep it looking casual, like you're just doing it for exercise."

Nels began throwing to Maxwell. He continued all during the *Morton's* time at bat, in which they were held scoreless. Mr. Buck watched from the bench with sad eyes.

"Sit down before Shorty comes back over here to the coaching box," Mr. Buck ordered. "I don't want him to see how much stuff you haven't got."

Feeling like the world's worst secret weapon, Nels sat down again and prayed that Carlson would last.

The *Iowa* got two more, and it was 10 to 8.

"I'll start the seventh," Carlson said gamely, "but the way it looks you'd better be ready with somebody."

Mr. Buck's thumb jerked in Nels's direction.

"Okay, Crane, warm up some more."

In the top of the seventh two men went down in order, but then Corny Schultz drove one between the left and center fielders, and Nels screamed with the rest for the redhead to make it all the way.

Corny did, by an eyelash, and the score was 11 to 8.

In the bottom of the seventh, the first man singled, and the second man walked. Mr. Buck went to the mound and confirmed his worst fears: Carlson had gone as far as he could go.

In his third-base coaching box, Shorty cupped his hands

and yelled: "How about it? Can we lend you that pitcher now?"

Mr. Buck ignored the needling. He signaled for a new pitcher.

Nels's legs quivered like the prongs of a tuning fork as he turned toward the mound. He didn't want to be the one who went out there and lost the game for this wonderful, cockeyed bunch of tin-can sailors, after they had come so close to a glorious victory over a battleship. Anything but that!

Oscar's wild-eyed face swam in front of him for an instant.

"Go get 'em, ol' buddy," Oscar yelled hoarsely, and gave him a shove in the right direction.

Wishing all the time that he were running the opposite way, Nels walked stiffly toward the mound where Carlson, Corny Schultz, and Mr. Buck were waiting. Carlson handed him the ball.

"Good luck, Crane. Keep 'em low and inside and you'll knock these guys off easy."

"That's right. Low and inside, Crane," agreed Mr. Buck. "Even without much stuff, if you can do that, we'll get by. Let 'em hit it, and we'll hope they keep it on the ground."

The manager and Carlson left the mound. Alone on that lonely eminence, Nels and Corny stood looking at each other.

"Well, this is the end," snorted Corny. *"You* again!"

He couldn't have picked anything better to say. It was

about the only remark in the world that could have made Nels grin at that moment.

"Come on, get back of the plate," he ordered. "I've got eight warm-up pitches coming."

Corny crouched behind the plate, and Nels began to throw. Watching from his box, Shorty was exultant.

"Okay, gang, let's go!" he yelled, planing his right hand toward center field. "Everybody hits!"

In the *Iowa's* dugout the enemy bench was roaring confidently. After the last warm-up pitch, Corny walked the ball out to the mound.

"Remember, low and inside. That's our only chance. The way you throw, anything else we give 'em will be curtains," he said bluntly.

The first batter stepped in. Nels looked down at Corny, settled behind the plate, and at the umpire leaning over behind him. The batter was lashing a bat back and forth the way a leopard, crouched to spring, lashes its tail. The bat looked as big as a mace, and the batter looked as big as Cousin Ludvig.

Nels hitched up his uncomfortable pants, glanced at the runners on first and second, stretched, and threw, low and inside. The batter swung. A sharp ground ball bounced straight at the shortstop, an easy double play ball.

Feeney bobbled it.

Everybody was safe. Scattering four-letter words through the warm night air like confetti, Feeney came to the mound and apologized.

"I'm sorry, kid. Don't let it rattle you."

"It's okay," said Nels. He turned to Corny, who had walked to the mound.

"Well, anyway, you put it in the right place," said Corny. "Low and inside."

"Yeah."

"Stay in there." Corny surprised him with a ballplayer's slap on the seat of his pants and waddled back behind the plate, awkward in his shinguards. Nels glanced from side to side and grinned wanly. *Bases loaded, score 11 to 8, winning run at the plate — and don't let it rattle you, he says.*

His first two pitches to the next batter were too low. The second pitch was almost in the dirt. In his anxiety not to throw one away, he grooved the next one right down the middle.

With a crack that sounded like one of the five-inchers, the batter laid the wood to it. In his third-base coaching box, Shorty danced and waved his arms for everybody to run. He had been waiting a long time for this moment. Numbly Nels squinted up to watch the ball. It was straight out to center field, and high. Doc was backing up under it, and now he was setting his feet as though in readiness for a quick throw.

Apparently it never occurred to Shorty or anybody else on the *Iowa* team that some little punk playing center field for a tin can would be able to hold on to a towering drive like that. This was a serious error of judgment. Doc gobbled the fly ball like a second Willy Mays, and got off a strike to the first baseman almost before the runners could skid to a stop and start scrambling back to their bases.

Nels's heart started beating again. Two down. Men on second and third. One more out now, and it would be in the books, the glorious victory of the U.S.S. *Morton* over the U.S.S. *Iowa*. Nels muttered a prayer.

"Lord, let me get this bum for the guys. Let me keep 'em low and inside."

The yelling now would have done justice to Ebbets Field. An entire softball team from the *New Jersey* had joined the ranks of those who were cheering for the *Morton*. Nels had never pitched under any kind of pressure before, and now the weight of the world seemed squarely on his shoulders. He gripped the horsehide, set his jaw, and tried for the inside corner.

It was an agonizing effort. Three times he tried for the corner and missed. The batter fouled off the next pitch. Then Nels missed once more, and the bases were loaded again.

Corny walked to the mound. Freckles stood out starkly all over his pale face. His red hair seemed more flaming than ever as he took off his cap and mopped his brow with his sleeve.

"I hate red hair," remarked Nels, grinning. The thorny eyebrows went up and down, and then Corny flashed a fierce grin in return. He recognized the crack for what it was — a smart attempt on Nels's part to relax them both a little in that tense moment.

"Okay, Lord Nelson. Just keep missing the corners, you bum, and you'll turn my hair gray. But be careful with this next guy."

"Who's he?"

234

"Nobody in particular. Just their clean-up man, that's all. Liable to hit one out of sight. So keep 'em low and inside, even if you have to walk him."

A grand slammer. Final score 12 to 11, favor of the *Iowa*. That was all they needed to ruin the evening for everyone. Nels blew out his breath and nodded.

"Let's try it."

The batter looked his first pitch over, and it was in there for a strike. Then Nels made him jump back with a tight pitch, and was low with his next two. The slugger hit a screamer down the third-base line on his following pitch, but it was foul, and the count was three and two.

Nels's face was streaming with sweat. He leaned forward and peered down at Corny. Low and inside. Make the batter hit it on the ground. It had to be in there this time, low and on the inside corner. He glanced at the runners dancing off their bases, went into his stretch, and put everything into a final pitch.

Never had he got more stuff on a ball. It was alive, it had a hop to it — but instead of staying low and inside, it took off. With the sort of helpless horror one feels in a nightmare, Nels watched the pitch travel high and outside, watched the batter set himself eagerly, watched him step into the pitch swinging from the heels . . .

WHISH!

Behind Corny, the umpire's arm went up.

"Stee-rike three! Yer out!"

For an instant Nels stood transfixed, open-mouthed, staring. Then he was deluged by destroyermen, hugging him, pounding his back, yelling in his ear. Mr. Faye and three other junior officers from the *Morton* were running back and forth from the refreshment stand with a round of beers for the team. Somebody handed him a beer. Corny Schultz planted himself in front of Nels and held up a beer can.

"Gentlemen," shouted Corny, "I give you Lord Nelson!"

"Lord Nelson!" roared the tattered band from the *Morton*. Corny put out his hand.

"Crane, you were the most."

Nels gripped his hand and returned the respect he saw in his one-time enemy's eyes. The impossible had happened: he didn't even mind his nickname any more.

"Brilliant, that's what it was!" declared Mr. Buck. "What a battery!"

"Oh, it was nothing." Corny winked at Nels and added an outrageous explanation. "I just called for a certain pitch, and Crane put it right where I asked for it. We had the bum figured all the way!"

After the game Oscar had one more irresistible suggestion up his sleeve: another swim. And as they floated around in the pool, reviewing the highlights of the game, he announced he was hungry again.

"Oh, boy. Here we go again," said Nels.

As they dressed, Nels explained his change of heart.

"I've decided she's not worth it. What's it to her if I wake up tomorrow with a miserable hangover? No, I've thought it all over, and I'm through with women. I wouldn't trust one again as far as I could see her. From now on I'm going

236

to be the happiest woman-hater you ever laid eyes on. Women! They're nothing but trouble."

Oscar was not pleased.

"What a thing to say. Honest, I don't know but what I'd rather see you get drunk than hear you talk thataway!"

# CHAPTER XIX

"CRANE," said Corny Schultz to the Strike-out King, as he was now known aboard the *Morton,* "I've been thinking about those two hours you owe me."

"Yes, sir?"

"I've thought of something I want you to do, the day we get back to the Academy. I believe you said you wouldn't be leaving until late afternoon or evening."

"That's correct, sir."

Corny took out a snapshot and handed it to Nels.

"You have my permission to shudder," he declared, as Nels looked at it. It was a color shot of a little girl about ten years old. She had bright red hair, and she was making a fresh face.

"A repulsive child, sir," remarked Nels. "Who is she?"

"My kid sister."

"I see, sir," nodded Nels without the slightest change of expression. "You have my sympathies."

"I need them. She is by all odds the freshest, most impudent brat, the biggest pest, the worst nuisance you've ever met. And you are going to meet her, because my family will be on hand for our homecoming. So brace yourself, Crane. Because what I want you to do is show her around the grounds of the Academy."

"Aye aye, sir."

"Well? Crane, I take my hat off to you. You didn't even flinch."

"Why should I, sir? The way I feel about women right now, a ten-year-old brat with poisonous red hair suits me fine. I, sir, am a woman-hater."

"Oh? After that experience in Hamburg, I'm not too sold on them myself. What happened to you?"

Nels explained. Even as he did so, a part of his mind was standing off and sputtering in amazement over the changes that had taken place in two months. It was incredible to think that he could ever talk so freely on so personal a matter to Corny Schultz, of all people — and find him a sympathetic audience.

"Crane, I can see your point," declared Corny, when Nels had finished. "After a deal like that, my sister Connie will be just your speed."

"I'll show her around, and buy her a comic book and an ice-cream cone afterwards," promised Nels. "By the way — you don't by any chance want to buy a set of the world's finest cashmere sweaters, size 34, do you?"

"With what?"

Nels nodded sadly. "That's what everyone says. Everyone's broke. I guess I'm stuck with them."

It was late, and they were standing on the fantail, enjoying the cool evening air after a sweltering hot day in the Gulf Stream, where a water temperature of 88°, a hot sun, and a following wind had combined to give them their most uncomfortable day of the entire cruise. As usual, Nels had sought out Corny to make his evening report.

Corny folded his arms now, pulled at his lower lip, and looked at Nels thoughtfully.

"Well, Crane, to all intents and purposes the cruise is over. Our cruise journals are completed, our work is done. So I think we can dispense with these morning and evening reports from here on in. I spoke to Mr. Jackson about it, and he agreed. In fact, he was kind enough to say he thought I had brought you along nicely, with some help from Tomlinson. He even went so far as to hint that Tomlinson and you would probably finish one-two on the youngster ladder, in that order."

Nels's heart flip-flopped at the words. He was too surprised to speak. He could only stare at Schultz.

"No joke," Corny assured him. "That's what he said." Corny grinned. "Who knows? Maybe you are another Lord Nelson, at that!"

Corny dismissed him then, and Nels toured the ship looking for Oscar to see if he had heard the incredible news. Nels's mind was whirling as it tried to adjust to this latest unexpected development. One minute he trembled with joy at the thought of how pleased his father would be, and the next minute his joy crumbled away as he realized that the promise he had shown would only make it that much harder for his father to understand how he could reject a career in the Navy.

Up forward, as he rounded the now dark and empty nav shack, he saw an officer step out of the inside passageway onto the deck. Even in silhouette, the ramrod military bearing was unmistakable. On an impulse, Nels quickened his pace and spoke.

"Good evening, Mr. Jackson."

"Evenin', Crane."

"Sir, may I speak with you for a moment?"

"Why, sure. What's on your mind, Crane?"

Mr. Jackson stood by the rail and looked at him keenly, while inside Nels a sharp struggle went on. He had approached the officer without quite knowing what he was going to say, but now he felt he could go no longer without laying his problem before somebody. He had to talk to somebody about it; he couldn't wrestle with it alone any more.

So he told Mr. Jackson the whole story. In a low tone, standing on the gently rolling ship in the velvety darkness, he poured it all out — his feelings about the way his father had been treated, his decision to resign from the Academy at the end of the cruise — everything.

The officer listened intently, and without interruption. When Nels had said it all, when he had finished and fallen silent, Mr. Jackson still said nothing for a moment, but stood looking out over the dark water at the twinkling lights of the great circular screen of ships, that familiar scene that had been the pattern of night for them for so long now.

241

"Well, Crane, maybe you think I'm going to give you the old Navy cheer, but I'm not," he began at last. "Every man who becomes an officer in the United States Navy takes a chance on havin' his heart broken seventeen different ways by it before he's through. Your father knew that, and he faced the fact right along, or he wouldn't have been able to take it the way he did when the tough breaks came.

"You blame the Navy, but the Navy only did what it had to do under the circumstances. That French expression, *C'est la guerre,* is something most people use as a joke, but it's no joke when you think about it. *C'est la guerre* — 'That's war.' Sure, your father should have been an admiral. But don't forget, he had a lot of classmates in the war who should be admirals now, too — only they didn't live to be. Your father at least lived, and he left a fine record behind him that every senior officer in the Navy knows about. You think Captain Penn doesn't know? Maybe he's never said a word to you, but more than once he's asked me, 'How's Captain Crane's boy coming along?' The really worthwhile things a man can chalk up in his life are a few basic things, like respect, and the respect of the whole U.S. Navy isn't somethin' every man earns."

He paused, and then shrugged.

"Well, I guess that's about the best I have to offer on the subject. You've only got one life. What you do with it should be your own decision. But whatever you do with it — good luck."

"Thank you, sir," said Nels, and the officer left him standing there beside the rail, staring into the darkness.

His struggling mind was filled with a kaleidoscope of images, jumbled and yet clear-cut, some bright, others somber. Faces and places flowed through his thoughts, unrelated and yet all woven together into the strange and wonderful texture of life: The expression on his mother's face when his father, dressed and ready to leave the hospital, picked up his cane for the first time. The perfect day in the English Channel, coming back, with the coasts of England and France clear and sharp under a brilliant sun that showed the white cliffs at their best. The *Morton* and *Wareham,* off Cuba, working together like two terriers in antisubmarine warfare exercises. Mule-hauling in rough seas with a queasy stomach. Painting the ship in a cold rain, getting her ready for port. Bangs's stubby fingers moving with strange grace as he demonstrated an eye splice while sitting on a bitt on the fo'c'sle. The bright, clean colors of Sweden in midsummer, and the sparkle in Kristine's level blue eyes. Eloise's fond and tearful good-by, an eternity ago. The captain on the bridge, collar turned up on his foul-weather jacket, his eyes laced at the corners with crow's-feet the sea had put there. . . .

It all went together, fitted together at strange angles and with unexpected juxtapositions, and all lent its colors, bright or somber, to the mood that kept him there by the rail, without moving, for a long, silent time.

They had sighted Chapel Dome as they came up Chesapeake Bay late the afternoon before; they were officially plebes no longer, but youngsters 100 per cent. Now, after a final night aboard, they were disembarking before dawn. The big motor launch had pulled away from the *Morton* and had become a dim outline on the black water.

On deck, watching the launch disappear, Bangs spat over the side.

"You know," he remarked to the grizzled chief bosun's mate, "I'm gonna miss that skinny young cornball."

In the launch, the cornball was sitting alongside Nels, just as he had been two months earlier.

"Well, Oscar, if I ever go to Europe again, I hope you'll be along to show me around," said Nels.

"Any time, ol' buddy, just call on me. Hey, look, I can see the landing now. Look at the gang waiting!"

Through the mist now, in the gray light of a sullen dawn, they could see the crowd of family and friends on hand to welcome them.

"What's that bunch of midshipmen doing there, all in a circle? Somebody faint, or something?" Oscar wondered as they neared the landing. Then the circle parted, and a tall, spectacularly well-built brunette hurried to the edge of the landing and peered at the approaching boatload of midshipmen. She began to wave wildly.

"Oscar Tomlinson, you sweet ol' thing!"

"Jumping gee-hosaphat, it's Claribel Hatch!" Oscar half-rose in his seat as though about to jump out of the boat. "Doggonit, I guess Cousin Ludvig couldn't hold her."

There was no escape for Oscar. When he clambered ashore Claribel gave him the mustard plaster treatment again while a hundred midshipmen watched and whistled enviously.

"Crane!"

It was Corny, summoning him imperiously.

"Crane, I want you to meet my sister Connie," he said.

Nels found himself looking into the hazel-green eyes of the prettiest redhead he had ever seen.

"I forgot to mention that my snapshot was taken seven years ago, but it's still my favorite picture of her," Corny went on to explain with a wicked chuckle. "Connie, this is Lord Nelson that I wrote you about. He's a woman-hater and he particularly dislikes red hair."

Connie's eyes glinted with a cool challenge that made Nels stammer in his haste to mend his fences.

"Well, there's red hair, and then there's red hair, and — well, I certainly hope you'll let me show you around the Academy, Connie."

She smiled then, and they made a date to meet later on. Nels went on his way wondering how yellow cashmere sweaters would look on a beautiful redhead, and was walking up the landing when the sight of his father, hurrying along as fast as his cane would allow him, stopped him in his tracks. He stared, and then broke into a run.

"Dad!"

"Hi, son!" The smile was bright and broad, with only the faintest hint of the dread that lay behind it. "I got squared away in Washington last night and thought I'd come on over here early. I almost made it at that, didn't I?"

Suddenly they were silent, facing each other, searching

245

each other's eyes. It was a moment Nels wanted to lay up like a treasure, a moment always to remember — that moment of doing something that would mean more to his father than anything else in the world.

"Dad," he said, "I'm staying in."